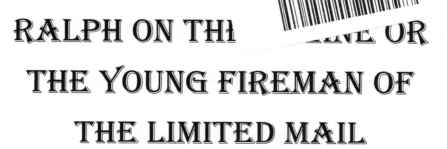

RALPH ON THE ENGINE OR

THE YOUNG FIREMAN OF

THE LIMITED MAIL

ALLEN CHAPMAN

Ralph On The Engine Or The Young Fireman Of The Limited Mail

CHAPTER I

THE NIGHT RUN

"Ralph Fairbanks."

"On hand, sir."

"You are to relieve Fireman Cooper on the Dover slow freight."

"All right, sir."

Ralph Fairbanks arose from the bench on which he was seated in the roundhouse at Stanley Junction.

Over a dozen men had been his companions for the past hour. There were engineers waiting for their runs, firemen resting after getting their locomotives in order, and "extras," who, like the young railroader himself, were so far on the substitute list only.

Ralph was glad of his appointment. This was his second month of service as a fireman. It had been by no means regular employment, and, as he was industrious and ambitious, he was glad to get at work with the prospect of a steady run.

The foreman of the roundhouse had just turned from his desk after marking Ralph's name on the list when a man hurriedly entered the place. He was rather unsteady in his gait, his face was flushed, and he looked dissolute and unreliable.

"Give me the slow freight run, Forgan," he panted. "I'm listed next."

"Two minutes late," observed the foreman, in a business-like way.

"That don't count on a stormy night like this."

"System counts in this establishment always, Jim Evans," said Mr. Forgan.

"I ran all the way."

"Stopped too long at the corner saloon, then," put in Dave Adams, a veteran engineer of the road.

Evans glared at the man who spoke, but recognizing a privileged character, stared down the row of loiterers and demanded:

"Who's got my run?"

"Do you own any particular run, Jim?" inquired Adams, with a grin.

"Well, Griscom's was due me."

"Young Fairbanks was on hand, so it's his run now."

"That kid's," sneered Evans, turning on Ralph with angry eyes. "See here, young fellow, do you think it's square cutting in on a regular man this way?"

"I'll answer that," interposed Tim Forgan sharply. "He was here, you weren't. He holds the run till a better man comes along."

Evans stood glaring at Ralph for a few minutes. Then he moved to the youth's side.

"See here, kid," he observed, "I want this run specially. It'll be a regular, for Cooper is going with another road. I'm a man and must earn a man's wages. You're only a kid. I've got a family. Come, give me the run and I'll treat you handsomely," and the speaker extended a cigar.

"Thank you, I don't smoke," said Ralph. Then looking the man squarely in the eyes, he said: "Mr. Evans, I'll give up the run on one condition."

"What's that?" inquired Evans eagerly.

"If you will sign the pledge, work steadily, and give your wages to your family as you should do."

"I'll do it!" shouted Evans, not a whit shame-facedly.

"No, you won't," announced Forgan. "Fairbanks, kindness is kindness, but business is business. If you drop this run, it goes to the next extra on the list according to routine."

"Bah, you're all down on me!" flared out Evans, and left the place in a rage.

"It would do no good, Fairbanks, to help that man," observed Dave Adams. "He would sign anything to secure a personal advantage and never keep his word. He squanders all his money and won't last long in the Great Northern, I can tell you."

Ralph went outside as he heard a whistle down the rails. Evans was standing near a switch.

"Some kind of a plot, eh, you and your friend?" he sneered at Ralph.

"I don't know what you mean, Mr. Evans," replied Ralph.

"Oh, yes, you do. Forgan is partial to you. The others don't like me because I'm a crack man in my line. One word, though; I'll pay you off for this some time or other," and Evans left the spot shaking his fist at Ralph menacingly.

"One of the bad kind," mused Ralph, looking after the fellow, "not at all fit for duty half the time. Here comes one of the good kind," he added as a freight engine with a long train of cars attached steamed up at the roundhouse. "It's my run, Mr. Griscom."

"That's famous news," cried old John Griscom, genuinely pleased.

"Good evening, Mr. Cooper," said Ralph, as the fireman leaped from the cab.

"Hello," responded the latter. "You got the run? Well, it's a good man in a good man's place."

"That's right," said Griscom. "None better. In to report, Sam? Good-bye. Shovel in the coal, lad," the speaker directed Ralph. "It's a bad night for railroading, and we'll have a hard run to Dover."

Ralph applied himself to his duties at once. He opened the fire door, and as the ruddy glow illuminated his face he was a picture pleasant to behold.

Muscular, healthy, in love with his work, friendly, earnest and accommodating, Ralph Fairbanks was a favorite with every fair-minded railroad man on the Great Northern who knew him.

Ralph had lived at Stanley Junction nearly all of his life. His early experiences in railroading have been related in the first volume of the present series, entitled "Ralph of the Roundhouse."

Ralph's father had been one of the pioneers who helped to build the Great Northern. When he died, however, it was found that the twenty thousand dollars' worth of stock in the road he was supposed to own had mysteriously disappeared.

Further, his home was mortgaged to old Gasper Farrington, a wealthy magnate of the village. This person seemed to have but one object in life; to drive the widow Fairbanks and her son from Stanley Junction.

Ralph one day overheard Farrington threaten to foreclose a mortgage, and the youth suddenly realized his responsibilities. Leaving school, he secured a job in the roundhouse at Stanley Junction. Here, notwithstanding the plots, hatred and malice of a worthless, good-for-nothing fellow named Ike Slump, whose place he took, Ralph made fine progress. He saved the railroad shops from wholesale destruction, by assisting John Griscom to run an engine into the flames and drive a car of powder out of the way. For this brave deed Ralph secured the friendship of the master mechanic of the road and was promoted to the position of junior leverman.

In the second volume of this series, entitled "Ralph in the Switch Tower," another vivid phase of his ability and merit has been depicted. He rendered signal service in saving a special from disaster and prevented a treasure train from being looted by thieves.

Among the thieves was his old-time enemy, Ike Slump, and a crony of his named Mort Bemis. They had been hired by Farrington to harass Ralph in every way possible. Ralph had searched for the motive to the old man's animosity.

He learned that Farrington had appropriated his father's railroad stock on an illegal technicality, and that the mortgage on their homestead had once been paid by Mr. Fairbanks.

Once knowing this, Ralph undertook the task of proving it. It required some clever work to unmask the villainous miser, but Ralph succeeded, and Farrington, to escape facing disgrace, left the town, ostensibly for Europe.

In unmasking the old man Ralph was assisted by one Van Sherwin, a poor boy whom he had befriended. Van and a former partner of Gasper Farrington, named Farwell Gibson, had secured a charter to build a short line railroad near Dover, in which project Ralph was very much interested.

As has been said, Ralph had now been a fireman for two months, but heretofore employed in yard service only.

"It's the chance of my life," he cried cheerily, as he piled in the coal, "and what a famous partner is dear, bluff, honest old John Griscom!"

"Won't have me for a partner long, lad," replied the veteran engineer with a slight sigh, as he moved the lever.

"Why not, Mr. Griscom?" inquired Ralph.

"Eyes giving out. Had to drop the Daylight Express. I'm going down the ladder, you are going up the ladder. Stick to your principles, lad, for they are good ones, as I well know, and you'll surely reach the top."

"I hope so." said Ralph.

The locomotive gave a sharp signal whistle, and the slow freight started on its night run for Dover.

CHAPTER II

THE LANDSLIDE

"Trouble ahead!"

"What's that, Fairbanks?"

"And danger. Quick! slow down, or we're in for a wreck."

Ralph Fairbanks spoke with suddenness. As he did so he leaped past the engineer in a flash, clearing the open window space at the side.

Two minutes previous the old engineer had asked him to go out on the locomotive to adjust some fault in the air gauge. Ralph had just attended to this when he made a startling discovery.

In an instant he was in action and landed on the floor of the cab. He sprang to his own side of the engine, and leaning far out peered keenly ahead.

They were now in a deep cut which ended a steep climb, and the engine had full steam on and was making fairly good speed.

"My bad eyes—" began Griscom, and then he quivered in every nerve, for a tremendous shock nearly sent him off his seat.

"Just in time," cried Ralph, and then he held his breath.

Slowing down, the train had come to a crashing halt. The locomotive reared upon its forward wheels and then settled back on a slant, creaking at every joint. Ralph had swung the air lever or there would have been a catastrophe.

"What was it?" gasped Griscom, clearing his old eyes and peering ahead, but Ralph was gone. Seizing a lantern, he had jumped to the ground and was at the front of the locomotive now. The engineer shut off all steam after sounding the danger signal, a series of several sharp whistles, and quickly joined his assistant.

In front of the locomotive, obstructing the rails completely, was a great mass of dirt, gravel and rocks.

"A landslide," spoke Griscom, glancing up one steep side of the cut.

"If we had struck that big rock full force," observed Ralph, "it would have been a bad wreck."

"You saved us just in time," cried the old engineer. "I've often wondered if some day there wouldn't be just such a drop as this of some of these overhanging cliffs. Company ought to see to it. It's been a fierce rain all the evening, perhaps that loosened the mass."

"Hardly," said Ralph thoughtfully, and then, inspecting a glazed piece of paper with some printing on it he had just picked up, he looked queerly at his companion.

"Give them the trouble signal in the caboose, please, Mr. Griscom," said the young fireman. "I think I had better get back there at once. Have you a revolver?"

"Always carry one," responded Griscom.

"Keep it handy, then."

"Eh!" cried the engineer with a stare. "What you getting at, lad?"

"That is no landslide," replied Ralph, pointing at the obstruction.

"What is it then?"

"Train wreckers—or worse," declared Ralph promptly. "There is no time to lose, Mr. Griscom," he continued in rapid tones.

"Of course, if not an accident, there was a purpose in it," muttered Griscom, reaching into his tool box for a weapon, "but what makes you think it wasn't an accident?"

Ralph did not reply, for he was gone. Springing across the coal heaped up in the tender, he climbed to the top of the first freight car and started on a swift run the length of the train.

The young fireman was considerably excited. He would not have been a spirited, wide-awake boy had he been otherwise. The paper he had found among the debris of the obstruction on the rails had an ominous sentence across it, namely, "Handle With Care, Dynamite."

This, taken in connection with what had at first startled him, made Ralph feel pretty sure that he had not missed his guess in attributing the landslide to some agency outside of nature.

While adjusting the air gauge Ralph had noticed a flare ahead, then a lantern light up the side of the embankment, and then, in the blaze of a wild flash of lightning, he had witnessed the descent of a great tearing, tossing mass, landing in the railroad cut.

"It can mean only a hold-up," theorized Ralph. "Yes, I am quite right."

He slowed down in his wild dash over the car tops, and proceeded with caution. Down at the end of the train he saw lights that he knew did not belong to the train hands.

Ralph neared the caboose and then dropped flat to the top of the car he was on. Peering past its edge, he made out a wagon, half-a-dozen men, and the

7

train hands backed to the side of the cut and held captive there by two of the strangers, who menaced them with revolvers.

Then two others of the marauding gang took crowbars from the wagon, and one, carrying a lantern, proceeded along the side of the cars inspecting the freight cards.

"They must know of some valuable goods on the train," reflected Ralph.

It was an ideal spot for a train robbery, between two stations, and no train was due for several hours.

Ralph was in a quandary as to his best course of procedure. For a moment he considered going for Griscom and arming himself with a bar of rod.

"It would be six to two and we would get the worst of it," he decided. "There is only one thing to do—get back to Brocton. It's less than a mile. Can I make it before these fellows get away with their plunder? Good! a patent coupler."

The boy fireman had crept to the end of the car next to the caboose. Glancing down, he discovered that the couplings were operated by a lever bar. Otherwise, he could never have forced up the coupling pin.

The cars were on a sharp incline, in fact, one of the steepest on the road. Ralph relied on simple gravity to escape the robbers and hasten for relief.

"There's some one!"

Careful as Ralph was, he was discovered. A voice rang out in warning. Then with a quick, bold snap, Ralph lifted the coupler and the pin shot out. He sprang to the forward platform of the caboose. As the car began to recede, he dashed through its open door.

"Just in time. Whew!" ejaculated Ralph, "those fellows are desperate men and doing this in true, wild western style."

The caboose, once started, began a rapid backward rush. Ralph feared that its momentum might carry the car from the track.

A curve turned, and the lights of Brocton were in sight. Before the runaway caboose slowed down entirely it must have gone fully three-quarters of a mile.

Ralph jumped from the car, and ran down the tracks at his best speed. He was breathless as he reached the little depot. It was dark and deserted, but opposite it was the one business street of the town.

Ralph left the tracks finally and made a dash for the open entrance of the general store of the village. The usual crowd of loiterers was gathered there.

"Hello! what's this?" cried the proprietor, as the young fireman rushed wildly into the store.

"Fireman on the Dover freight," explained Ralph breathlessly.

"What's the trouble—a wreck?"

"No, a hold-up. Men! get weapons, a handcar, if there is one here, and we may head off the robbers."

It took some urging to get that slow crowd into action, but finally half-a-dozen men armed with shotguns were running down the tracks following Ralph's lead.

It was a steep climb and several fell behind, out of breath. One big fellow kept pace with Ralph.

"There they are," spoke the latter as they rounded a curve.

Lights showed in the near distance. A flash of lightning momentarily revealed a stirring scene. The robbers were removing packages from a car they had broken into, and these they were loading into their wagon at the side of the train.

"Hurry up, hurry up!" Ralph's companion shouted back to his comrades. "Now, then, for a dash, and we'll bag those rogues, plunder, rig and all."

"Wait," ordered Ralph sharply.

He was too late. The impetuous villager was greatly excited and he ran ahead and fired off his gun, two of the others following his example.

Ralph was very sorry for this, for almost instantly the robbers took the alarm and all lights near the caboose were extinguished. The echo of rapid orders reached the ears of the relief party. Fairly upon the scene, a flash of lightning showed the wagon being driven rapidly up a road leading from the cut.

"Look out for yourselves," suggested Ralph. "Those men are armed."

"So are we, now!" sharply sounded the voice of one of the men from Brocton, and another flash of lightning showed the enemy still in view.

"Up the road after them!" came a second order.

Ralph ran up to the side of the caboose.

"All safe?" he inquired anxiously.

"All but one of us," responded the conductor.

Ralph lit a lantern, noticing one of the train hands lying on the ground motionless.

"He's a fighter, Tom is," said the conductor. "He resisted and grappled with one of the robbers, and another of them knocked him senseless."

"What's this in his hand?" inquired Ralph. "Oh, I see—a cap. Snatched it from the head of his assailant, I suppose. Hark! they are shooting up there."

Shots rang out along the cut road. In a few minutes, however, the men from Brocton reappeared in the cut.

"No use wasting our lives recklessly," said one of them. "They have bullets, we only small shot. The wagon got away. We'll hurry back to Brocton, get a regular posse armed with rifles, and search the country for the rascals."

"What's the damage?" inquired Ralph of the conductor, going to the side of the car that had been broken open.

"Pretty big, I should say," responded the conductor. "That car had a consignment of valuable silks from Brown & Banks, in the city, and they piled a fair load of it into their wagon. You have saved a wholesale plundering of the car."

The men from Brocton departed. Ralph helped the train crew revive the poor fellow who had been knocked insensible. They carried him into the caboose, applied cold water to his head, and soon had him restored to consciousness.

"Fix the red lights," ordered the conductor to a brakeman, "and then hurry to Brocton and have them telegraph the train dispatcher. What's the trouble ahead, Fairbanks?"

Ralph explained. Shovels and crowbars were brought from the caboose, and two of the train crew accompanied him back to the locomotive.

Ralph thought of the cap he had stuck in his pocket. He looked it over carefully in the light of the lantern he carried.

On the leather band inside of the cap were two initials in red ink—"I. S."

"Ike Slump," murmured Ralph.

An old-time enemy had appeared on the scene, and the young fireman of the Great Northern knew that he would have to keep a sharp lookout or there would be more trouble.

CHAPTER III

EVERYBODY'S FRIEND

"Stand back there, you fellows!"

"Scatter, boys—it's Ralph Fairbanks!"

It was two days after the landslide near Brocton. The young fireman had just left the roundhouse at Stanley Junction in a decidedly pleasant mood. His cheering thoughts were, however, rudely disturbed by a spectacle that at once appealed to his manly nature.

Ralph, making a short cut for home, had come across a farmer's wagon standing in an alley at the side of a cheap hotel. The place was a resort for dissolute, good-for-nothing railway employes, and one of its victims was now seated, or rather propped up, on the seat of the wagon in question.

He was a big, loutish boy, and had apparently come into town with a load to deliver. The wagon was filled with bags of apples. Around the vehicle was gathered a crowd of boys. Each one of them had his pockets bulging with the fruit stolen from one of the bags in the wagon.

Standing near by, Jim Evans in their midst, was an idle crowd of railroad men, enjoying and commenting on the scene.

The farmer's boy was seemingly asleep or unconscious. He had been set up on the seat by the mob, and one side of his face blackened up. Apples stuck all over the harness of the horses and on every available part of the vehicle. A big board lying across the bags had chalked upon it, "Take One."

The crowd was just about to start this spectacle through the public streets of Stanley Junction when Ralph appeared. The young fireman brushed them aside quickly, removed the adornments from the horses and wagon, sprang to the vehicle, threw the sign overboard, and, lifting up the unconscious driver, placed him out of view under the wagon seat. As he did so, Ralph noticed the taint of liquor on the breath of the country lad.

"Too bad," he murmured to himself. "This doesn't look right—more like a piece of malice or mischief. Stand back, there!"

Ralph took up the reins, and also seized the whip. Many of the crowd he had known as school chums, and most of them drew back shamefacedly as he appeared.

There were four or five regular young loafers, however, who led the mob. Among them Ralph recognized Ted Evans, a son of the fireman he had encountered at the roundhouse two days previous. With him was a fellow named Hemp Gaston, an old associate of Mort Bemis.

"Hold on, there!" sang out Gaston, grabbing the bridles of the horses. "What you spoiling our fun for?"

"Yes," added Ted Evans, springing to the wagon step and seizing Ralph's arm. "Get off that wagon, or we'll pull you off."

Ralph swung the fellow free of the vehicle with a vigorous push.

"See here, you interfere with my boy and I'll take a hand in this affair myself," growled Jim Evans, advancing from the crowd of men.

"You'll whip me first, if you do," answered one of them. "This is a boys' squabble, Jim Evans, and don't you forget it."

"Humph! he struck my boy."

"Then let them fight it out."

"Yes," shouted young Evans angrily, "come down here and show that you are no coward."

"Very well," said Ralph promptly. "There's one for you!"

Ralph Fairbanks had acted in a flash on an impulse. He had leaped from the wagon, dealt young Evans one blow and sent him half-stunned to the ground. Regaining the wagon he drove quickly into the street before his astonished enemies could act any further.

"Poor fellow," said Ralph, looking at the lad in the wagon. "Now, what am I ever going to do with him?"

Ralph reflected for a moment or two. Then he started in the direction of home. He was sleepy and tired out, and he realized that the present episode might interfere with some of his plans for the day, but he was a whole-hearted, sympathetic boy and could not resist the promptings of his generous nature.

The young fireman soon reached the pretty little cottage that was his home, so recently rescued from the sordid clutches of old Gasper Farrington. He halted the team in front of the place and entered the house at once.

"Here I am, mother," he said cheerily.

Mrs. Fairbanks greeted him with a smile of glad welcome.

"I was quite anxious about you when I heard of the wreck, Ralph," she said with solicitude. He had not been home since that happening.

"It was not a wreck, mother," corrected Ralph. Then he briefly recited the incidents of the hold-up.

"It seems as though you were destined to meet with all kinds of danger in your railroad life," said the widow. "You were delayed considerably."

"Yes," answered Ralph, "we had to remove the landslide debris. That took us six hours and threw us off our schedule, so we had to lay over at Dover all day yesterday. One pleasant thing, though."

"What is that, Ralph?"

"The master mechanic congratulated me this morning on what he called, 'saving the train.'"

"Which you certainly did, Ralph. Why, whose wagon is that in front of the house?" inquired Mrs. Fairbanks, observing the vehicle outside for the first time.

Ralph explained the circumstances of his rescue of the vehicle to his mother.

"What are you going to do with the farmer's boy?" she inquired.

"I want to bring him in the house until he recovers."

"Very well, I will make up a bed on the lounge for him," said the woman. "It is too bad, poor fellow! and shameful—the mischief of those men at the hotel."

Ralph carried the farmer's boy into the house. Then he ate his breakfast. After the meal was finished, he glanced at his watch.

"I shall have to lose a little sleep, mother," he said. "I am anxious to help the poor fellow out, and I think I see a way to do it."

The young fireman had noticed a small blank book under the cushion of the wagon seat. He now inspected it for the first time. All of its written pages were crossed out except one. This contained a list of names of storekeepers in Stanley Junction.

Ralph drove to the store first named in the list. Within two hours he had delivered all of the apples. It seemed that the storekeepers named in the account book ordered certain fruits and vegetables regularly from the owner of the team, the farmer himself coming to town to collect for the same twice each month.

When Ralph got back home he unhitched the horses, tied them up near the woodshed, and fed them from a bag of grain he found under the wagon seat.

"What is this, I wonder?" he said, discovering a small flat parcel under the wagon seat. The package resembled a store purchase of some kind, so, for safe keeping, Ralph placed it inside the shed.

His mother had gone to visit a sick neighbor. The farmer boy was sleeping heavily.

"Wake me before the boy leaves," he wrote on a card, leaving this for his mother on the kitchen table. Then, pretty well tired out, Ralph went to bed.

It was late in the afternoon when he awoke. He went down stairs and glanced into the sitting room.

"Why, mother," he exclaimed, "where is the farmer boy?"

"He left two hours ago, Ralph."

"Is that so? Then why didn't you wake me up? I left a card for you on the kitchen table."

"I did not find it," said the widow, and then a search revealed the card where the wind had blown it under the stove.

"What did the boy say?" inquired Ralph.

"He told me his name was Zeph Dallas. I talked to him about his misfortunes of the morning, and he broke down and cried. Then he went out to the wagon. He found an account book there, and said you must have delivered his load for him, and that he would never forget your kindness."

"There was a package in the wagon," said Ralph.

"He spoke of that, and said some one must have stolen it."

"You are sure he didn't find it later?" inquired Ralph. "It was in the woodshed, where I placed it for safe keeping."

Ralph went out to the shed, and found the package where he had left it. He returned to the house with it, ate a hurried meal, and hastened down town. He learned that Zeph had called at several stores. The farmer boy appeared to have discovered Ralph's interest in his behalf, and had driven home.

"I wonder what there is in the package?" mused Ralph, when he again reached the cottage. "I had better open it and find out."

The young fireman was quite startled as he untied the parcel and glanced at its contents. The package contained two bolts of silk, and the tags on them bore the name of the firm which, Ralph had learned at Dover, had shipped the goods stolen from the slow freight two nights previous.

CHAPTER IV

AN OLD-TIME ENEMY

"New engine, lad?"

"Not at all, Mr. Griscom, as you well know," answered Ralph.

The veteran engineer chuckled, but he continued looking over the locomotive with admiring eyes.

The young fireman had come to work early that afternoon. The roundhouse men were careless and he decided to show them what "elbow grease" and industry could do. In an hour he had the old freight locomotive looking indeed like a new engine.

They steamed out of the roundhouse and were soon at the head of their freight train.

"I wish I had a little time to spare," said Ralph.

"Half-an-hour before we have to leave, you know, lad," said Griscom. "What's troubling you?"

"I wanted to see Bob Adair, the road detective."

"About the silk robbery?" inquired the engineer with interest.

"Yes."

"Something new?"

"Considerable, I think."

"You might find him in the depot offices. Run down and see. I'll attend to things here."

"Thanks, Mr. Griscom."

Ralph hurried away from the freight train. He wished to report about the discovery of the silk, and hunt up Zeph Dallas at once.

"I hardly believe the farmer boy a thief," mused Ralph, "but he must explain his possession of that silk."

The young fireman did not find Adair at the depot, and came back to the engine to discover Jim Evans lounging in the cab.

"Been helping Griscom out," grinned the man.

"Well, get out, now," growled Griscom. "Time to start up. There's the signal from the conductor. That man has been hanging around the engine ever since you left," the old engineer continued to Ralph, "and he is too good-natured to suit me."

"Nothing out of order," reported the youth, looking about the cab.

"Now, lad, for a run on time," said Griscom. "This run has been late a good deal, and I don't want to get a bad name. When I ran the Daylight Express it was my pride and boast that we were always on time to the minute."

They made good time out of Stanley Junction to Afton. Ten miles beyond, however, there was a jolt, a slide and difficult progress on a bit of upgrade rails.

So serious was the difficulty that Griscom stopped the train and got out to investigate. He returned to the cab with a set, grim face.

"Grease," he reported; "some one has been tampering with the rails. Spite work, too."

There was fully an hour's delay, but a liberal application of sand to the rails helped them out. Five miles later on the locomotive began to puff and jerk. With full steam on, the engine did only half duty.

"Water gauge all right," said Ralph. "I don't understand it."

"I do," said Griscom, "and I can tell it in two words—Jim Evans."

"Why, what do you mean, Mr. Griscom?"

"He didn't come into the cab for nothing. Yes, we are victims of the old trick—soap in the water and the valves are clogged."

"What are we going to do about it?" inquired Ralph anxiously.

"Pump out the water at the next tank and take a new supply on."

There was a further delay of nearly two hours. Once more they started up. Ten miles from Dover, a few seconds after Ralph had thrown in coal, a terrible explosion threw the fire cover open and singed and burned both engineer and fireman.

Griscom looked angry, for the fire now needed mending.

"Lad," he said grimly, "these tricks are done to scare you and delay the train."

"I am not scared one particle," retorted Ralph, "only this strikes me as a dangerous piece of mischief—putting explosives in among the coal."

"Jim Evans did it," positively asserted Griscom. "That's what he sneaked into the cab for, and he has confederates along the line."

Ralph said nothing but he resolved to call Evans to account when he returned to Stanley Junction.

They were over an hour late on the run. Returning to Stanley Junction, they were delayed by a wreck and the time record was bad at both ends of the line.

16

"I don't like it," said Griscom.

"We'll mend it, Mr. Griscom," declared the young fireman, and he did not go home when they reached Stanley Junction, but proceeded at once to the home of Jim Evans.

Ralph knocked at the open door, but no one answered the summons and he stepped to the door of the sitting room.

"Any one here?" he called out through the house.

"Eh? oh—no," answered a muffled voice, and a man in the adjoining room got up quickly and fairly ran out through the rear door.

"That's queer," commented Ralph. "That man actually ran away from me."

"Ma has gone after pa," lisped a little urchin in the kitchen. "Man wants to see him. What for funny man run away?"

Ralph hurried past the infantile questioner and after the object of his curiosity.

"Yes, the man did look funny, for a fact," said Ralph. "He was disguised. There he is. Hey, there! whoever you are, a word with you."

He was now in close pursuit of a scurrying figure. The object of his curiosity turned to look at him, stumbled, and went headlong into a ditch.

Ralph came to the spot. The man lay groaning where he had fallen.

"Help me," he muttered—"I'm nearly stunned."

"Why!" exclaimed Ralph as he assisted the man to his feet, "it is Gasper Farrington."

It was the village magnate, disguised. He stood regarding Ralph with savage eyes.

"I thought you had gone to Europe, Mr. Farrington," said Ralph.

"Did you? Well, I haven't," growled Farrington, nursing a bruise on his face.

"Are you going to stay in Stanley Junction, then?"

"None of your business."

"Oh, yes, it is," retorted Ralph quickly. "You owe us thousands of dollars, and we want it."

"You'll collect by law, then. I'll never give you a cent willingly."

Ralph regarded the man thoughtfully for a minute or two.

"Mr. Farrington," he said, "I have come to the conclusion that you are trying to make me more trouble. This man Evans is up to mischief, and I believe that you have incited him to it."

17

The magnate was silent, regarding Ralph with menacing eyes.

"I warn you that it won't pay, and that you won't succeed," continued Ralph. "What do you hope to accomplish by persecuting me?"

The old man glanced all about him. Then he spoke out.

"Fairbanks," he said, "I give you one last chance—get out of Stanley Junction."

"Why should I?" demanded Ralph.

"Because you have humiliated me and we can't live in the same town together, that's why."

"You deserved humiliation," responded Ralph steadily.

"All right, take your own view of the case. I will settle your claim for five thousand dollars and pay you the money at once, if you will leave Stanley Junction."

"We will not take one cent less than the full twenty thousand dollars due us," announced Ralph staunchly, "and I shall not leave Stanley Junction as long as my mother wants to live here."

"Then," said Gasper Farrington, venomously, as he walked from the spot, "look out for yourself."

Ralph went back to the Evans home, but found only the little child there. He concluded he would not wait for Evans that evening. The discovery of his old-time enemy, Farrington, had been enlightening.

"I will have a talk with mother about this," he mused.

When Ralph reached home a surprise greeted him. The little parlor was lighted up, indicating a visitor. He glanced in through the open windows.

The visitor was Zeph Dallas, the farmer boy.

CHAPTER V

ON SPECIAL DUTY

Ralph entered the house glad of an opportunity to interview the farmer boy, who had been in his thoughts considerably during the day.

"Mr. Dallas, this is my son, Ralph," said Mrs. Fairbanks, as the young fireman came into the parlor.

The visitor arose from his chair in an awkward, embarrassed fashion. He flushed and stammered as he grasped Ralph's extended hand.

"Brought you a sack of potatoes and some apples," he said. "Neighbor gave me a lift in his wagon."

"Is that so?" returned Ralph with a friendly smile. "Well, Mr. Dallas, I am very glad to see you."

"Gladder than you were last time, I reckon," said Zeph. "Say, I—I want to say I am ashamed of myself, and I want to thank you for all you did for me. It's made me your friend for life, so I came to ask a favor of you."

This was rather a queer way of putting the case, thought Ralph, and the fellow blundered on.

"You see, Mr. Ames, that's the man who hired me, found out about my doings down here at Stanley Junction, and he has set me adrift."

"That is too bad," observed Ralph.

"No, it ain't, for I deserve better work," dissented Zeph. "They say you're dreadfully smart and everybody's friend, and I want you to help me get where I want to get."

"All right, I am willing to try to assist you."

"I don't know exactly which I had better do," proceeded Zeph—"become a chief of police or a railroad conductor. Of course, the man who speaks quickest and will pay the most money gets me."

Ralph concealed a smile, for Zeph was entirely in earnest.

"Well, you see," remarked the young fireman, "it is somewhat difficult to get just the position you want without some experience."

"Oh, that's all right," declared the farmer boy confidently. "I've thought it all out. I once watched a conductor go through a train. Why, it's no work at all. I could do it easily. And as to being a detective I've read lots of books on the subject, and I've even got some disguises I made up, in my satchel here."

"Oh, brought your satchel, too, did you?" observed Ralph.

19

"Why, yes, I thought maybe you'd house me for a day or two till I closed a contract with somebody."

The fellow was so simple-minded that Mrs. Fairbanks pitied him, and, observing this, Ralph said:

"You are welcome, Zeph, and I will later talk over with you the prospects of a situation."

The visitor was soon completely at home. He ate a hearty supper, and, after the meal, took some home-made disguises from his satchel. The poor fellow strutted around proudly as he put these on in turn.

"Old peddler," he announced, donning a skull cap, a white beard made out of rope, and a big pair of goggles. "Tramp," and he put on a ragged coat and a torn cap, and acted out the appearance of a typical tramp quite naturally. There were several other representations, but all so crude and funny that Ralph with difficulty restrained his merriment.

"How will it do?" inquired Zeph, at the conclusion of the performance.

"You have got the elements of the profession in mind," said Ralph guardedly, "but there is the practical end of the business to learn."

Then Ralph seriously and earnestly told his visitor the real facts of the case. He devoted a full hour to correcting Zeph's wrong impressions of detective and railroad work. By the time he got through, Zeph's face was glum.

"Why, if what you say is true," he remarked dejectedly, "I'm next to being good for nothing."

"Oh, no," said Ralph, "don't you be discouraged at all. You have the starting point of every ambition—an idea. I myself do not think much of the detective line for one as young as you are. As to railroading, I can tell you one fact."

"What's that?" interrogated Zeph dreamily.

"You must begin at the bottom of the ladder and take one step at a time— slow steps, sure steps, to reach the top."

"You're a fireman, aren't you?" asked Zeph, admiringly.

Ralph answered that he was, and this led to his relating to the curious and interested Zeph the story of his career from roundhouse worker and switch tower man to the present position.

"It's fascinating, ain't it?" said Zeph, with a long-drawn breath, when Ralph concluded his recital. "I reckon I'll give up the detective idea. Can you help me get a position in the roundhouse?"

"I am willing to try," assented Ralph. "You are strong and used to hard work, and that means a good deal in the roundhouse service."

Ralph suggested a stroll before bedtime. Zeph was glad for the exercise. Once they were outside, Ralph broached a subject he had been thinking over all the evening.

"Zeph," he said, "I want to ask you a very important question."

"What is that?"

"You remember the day I kept your team for you?"

"I'll never forget it."

"You missed a package that had been under the feed bags when you came to leave town?"

"Yes, and that's why I am here," said Zeph. "Old Ames was almost ready to discharge me for letting those men at the hotel give me drink I had never tasted before and getting in that fix you found me in, and for losing some of the apples, but when he found out that I had lost that package, he was nearly wild."

"Was there something so valuable in it, then?"

"I dunno. I only know I was told to be sure I kept it hidden and safe till it was delivered to a fellow named Evans in town here."

"Jim Evans?"

"Yes, that's the full name."

Ralph looked pretty serious.

"You see, old Ames himself didn't send the package," went on Zeph. "It was brought to the house by a fellow who had hired a team from Ames one day last week. Dunno who he is, dunno where he lives, but I can describe him, if you are interested."

"I am interested, very much so," assented Ralph.

Zeph went on to describe the person he had alluded to. By the time he had concluded, it was evident to Ralph that the sender of the package was Ike Slump.

The young fireman took Zeph back to the house but did not enter it himself.

"I will be back soon, Zeph," he said, "I have some business down town."

Ralph went at once to the home of Bob Adair.

"Want to see me, Fairbanks?" questioned the brisk, wide-awake railroad detective, as Ralph was shown into the room where he was busily engaged in packing a satchel.

"Yes, Mr. Adair, about the silk robbery."

"Oh, that mystery," nodded the detective. "I spent two days on it, and didn't find a clew."

"I had one, but failed to find you," explained Ralph. "I'll tell you all about it now."

"Quick work, then, Fairbanks," went on Adair, "for I'm due for a special to the city. Big case from the General Superintendent."

Ralph rapidly related all he had learned. Adair listened intently. He reflected for a moment or two after the young fireman had finished his recital. Then he said:

"Fairbanks, this is of great importance, but I can't neglect the city case. You helped me on another similar case once."

"Yes," said Ralph.

"Also aided me in running down those switch tower wreckers."

Ralph nodded.

"Good work, and you did nobly in those affairs. Let me think. Yes, I'll do it! Here, I want you to go straight to the Assistant Superintendent at Afton."

"You mean to-night?"

"Right away. I will give you a letter. No, hold on, I've got a better plan."

Again Adair consulted his watch. Bustlingly he hurried through with his preparations for departure. Then he left the house, swung down the street briskly, and, Ralph accompanying him, proceeded to the railroad depot.

He wrote out a long telegram and handed it to the night operator. Then he came back to Ralph.

"See here, Fairbanks," he remarked. "I've fixed this thing as I want it, and you are one of the few persons I would trust in a matter like this."

"Thank you for the compliment, Mr. Adair."

"I know your ability from past experience. It won't do to neglect following this clew to the silk robbers. I have wired the assistant superintendent for an official request that you be detailed on special duty in my department. Wait here for the reply. Then start out on the trail of those thieves, and report to me day after to-morrow, when I shall return to Stanley Junction."

"All right," said Ralph, "I may be able to accomplish something."

"I think you will, judging from your present success in assisting me," said Adair.

22

Ralph had to wait nearly an hour after Adair had left on a special. Then a reply came to the telegram. The operator, as instructed by Adair, handed the message to Ralph. It read:

"Fairbanks, freight fireman, detailed for special work in another department."

"It's all right," said Ralph to himself, as he started homewards. "Now to trace down Ike Slump and the other train robbers."

CHAPTER VI

ZEPH

The young fireman reported at the roundhouse early in the morning, showing the telegram to Jim Forgan, but not until the foreman had got out of sight and hearing of the other men in the place.

"H'm!" commented Forgan laconically, "I don't like this."

"Indeed, Mr. Forgan?" smiled Ralph.

"I don't, and that's the truth of it—for two reasons."

"What are they, Mr. Forgan?"

"First, it interrupts a regular run for you."

"But I may not be away two days."

"Next, it gives that Jim Evans a chance to take your place, and I don't trust the man."

"Neither do I," said Ralph pointedly, "and I may have something important to tell you about him when I return."

Ralph found Zeph industriously chopping kindling wood when he got back home again. The young fireman went into the house, explained his new employment to his mother, and then called to Zeph.

"You wanted some work, Zeph," he said to the farmer boy.

"Sure, I do," cried Zeph with unction.

"Very well, I think I am authorized to offer you a dollar a day."

"Steady job?" inquired Zeph eagerly.

"No, it may not last, but it is in the railroad service, and may lead to your further employment."

"Good," commented Zeph. "What do they want me to do—engineer?"

"Scarcely, Zeph," said Ralph, smiling. "I simply want you to take me back to the Ames farm and direct me about the locality."

Zeph looked disappointed.

"Why, what's that kind of work got to do with railroading?" he said.

"You shall know later."

"All right. You're too smart to make any mistakes and too friendly to do anything but good for me, so I'm your man."

"Very well. First, then, tell me the location of the Ames farm."

24

Zeph did this, and Ralph ascertained that it was about five miles west of Brocton.

Ralph secured some money, and in an hour he and Zeph stepped aboard the cab of a locomotive attached to a load of empties due to run down the line in a few minutes.

They reached Brocton about noon. Ralph proceeded down the tracks towards the railroad cut which had been the scene of the landslide.

He turned off at the wagon road and soon, with his companion, was started westward in the direction of the Ames farm.

"Zeph," he said, "did you hear anything of a train robbery here the other night?"

No, Zeph had not heard of it. Then Ralph questioned him closely as to the night Ames had loaned his wagon to strangers and gained a few more particulars relating to the silk robbers.

"There is the Ames farm," reported Zeph at last.

Ralph had already planned out what he would do, and proceeded to instruct his assistant as to his share in the affair.

"Zeph," he said, "I do not wish to be seen by Ames, nor must he know that you came here with a stranger."

"Am I to see him?"

"Yes," answered Ralph, taking a package from under his coat.

"Why, that's the package I lost!" cried Zeph.

"The same."

"And you had it all the time?"

"I did, Zeph, yes. No mystery about it—I simply don't care to explain to you anything about it till a little later on."

"All right."

"I want you to take it and go up to the farmhouse. I will keep out of sight. You go to Ames and tell him it was returned to you, and you want to give it back to the person it belongs to with a message."

"Whose message?"

"Nobody's," answered Ralph, "but you need not say that."

"What shall I say, then?"

"Tell him you want to advise the person who sent the parcel that it isn't safe to send such goods to any one at the present time."

"Very well," said Zeph. "Suppose Ames tells me where to find the fellow who sent the package?"

"Come back and report to me."

Zeph started for the farmhouse. Ralph watched him enter it, the package in his hand. He came out in a very few minutes without the parcel.

He was rather glum-faced when he rejoined Ralph.

"Say," he observed, "I've found out nothing, and old Ames took the package away from me."

"What did he say?" asked the young fireman.

"He told me he would see that it was returned to the person who sent it."

"That delays matters," thought Ralph, "and I don't know whether Ames will take it back to the silk thieves, or wait for some of them to visit him."

Then the young fireman formed a sudden resolution. He regarded his companion thoughtfully, and said:

"Zeph, I am going to trust you with what is known as an official secret in the railroad line."

The farmer boy looked pleased and interested.

"I believe you are too square and friendly to betray that secret."

"Try me, and see!" cried Zeph with ardor.

"Well," said Ralph, "there was a silk robbery of the Dover night freight last week, the train I am fireman on. From what you have told me, I feel sure that the thieves hired their rig from Ames. That package you had was part of the stolen plunder. I am acting for the road detective of the Great Northern, and I must locate those robbers."

"Then," cried Zeph delightedly, "I am helping you do detective work."

"Yes, Zeph, genuine detective work."

"Oh! how I wish I had my disguises here!"

"You are of more use to me as you are, because the thieves know you worked for Ames, and they seem to trust him."

"That's so," said Zeph thoughtfully. "What you going to do?"

"I want to locate the thieves," responded Ralph. "You must know the district about here pretty well. Can't you think of any spot where they would be likely to hide?"

"None in particular. But I know every foot of the woods, swamps and creek. If the men you are looking for are anywhere in the neighborhood, I am sure we will find a trace of them."

"You pilot the way, then, Zeph. Go with caution if you find any traces of the men, for I am sure that at least two of the party know me."

For three hours they made a tour of the district, taking in nearly four miles to the south. The swamp lands they could not traverse. Finally they came out of the woods almost directly on a town.

"Why," said Ralph in some surprise, "here is Millville, the next station to Brocton."

"That's so," nodded Zeph. "I hardly think those fellows are in the woods. We have made a pretty thorough search."

"There's the swamp and the high cliffs we haven't visited," said Ralph. "I suppose you are hungry?"

"Moderately," answered Zeph.

"Then we will go and have something to eat. I have a friend just on the edge of Millville, who keeps a very unique restaurant."

Ralph smiled pleasantly, for the restaurant in question was quite a feature with railroad men.

Two lines of railroad crossed at Millville, a great deal of switching was done outside of the town, and there was a shanty there to shelter the men.

A little off from the junction was a very queer-looking house, if it could be called such. Its main structure was an old freight car, to which there had been additions made from time to time. Across its front was a sign reading, "Limpy Joe's Railroad Restaurant."

"Ever taken a meal here?" inquired Ralph, as they approached the place.

"No."

"Ever heard of Limpy Joe?"

"Don't think I have."

"Then," said Ralph, "I am going to introduce you to the most interesting boy you ever met."

CHAPTER VII

LIMPY JOE'S RAILROAD RESTAURANT

Zeph Dallas stared about him in profound bewilderment and interest as Ralph led the way towards Limpy Joe's Railroad Restaurant.

It was certainly an odd-appearing place. Additions had been built onto the freight car until the same were longer than the original structure.

A square of about two hundred feet was enclosed by a barbed wire fence, and this space was quite as interesting as the restaurant building.

There was a rude shack, which seemed to answer for a barn, a haystack beside it, and a well-appearing vegetable garden. Then, in one corner of the yard, was a heap of old lumber, stone, brick, doors, window sash, in fact, it looked as if some one had been gathering all the unmated parts of various houses he could find.

The restaurant was neatly painted a regular, dark-red freight-car color outside. Into it many windows had been cut, and a glance through the open doorway showed an interior scrupulously neat and clean.

"Tell me about it," said Zeph. "Limpy Joe—who is he? Does he run the place alone?"

"Yes," answered Ralph. "He is an orphan, and was hurt by the cars a few years ago. The railroad settled with him for two hundred dollars, an old freight car and a free pass for life over the road, including, Limpy Joe stipulated, locomotives and cabooses."

"Wish I had that," said Zeph—"I'd be riding all the time."

"You would soon get tired of it," Ralph asserted. "Well, Joe invested part of his money in a horse and wagon, located in that old freight car, which the company moved here for him from a wreck in the creek, and became a squatter on that little patch of ground. Then the restaurant idea came along, and the railroad hands encouraged him. Before that, however, Joe had driven all over the country, picking up old lumber and the like, and the result is the place as you see it."

"Well, he must be an ambitious, industrious fellow."

"He is," affirmed Ralph, "and everybody likes him. He's ready at any time of the night to get up and give a tired-out railroad hand a hot cup of coffee or a lunch. His meals are famous, too, for he is a fine cook."

"Hello, Ralph Fairbanks," piped a happy little voice as Ralph and Zeph entered the restaurant.

Ralph shook hands with the speaker, a boy hobbling about the place on a crutch.

"What's it going to be?" asked Limpy Joe, "full dinner or a lunch?"

"Both, best you've got," smiled Ralph. "The railroad is paying for this."

"That so? Then we'll reduce the rates. Railroad has been too good to me to overcharge the company."

"This is my friend, Zeph Dallas," introduced Ralph.

"Glad to know you," said Joe. "Sit down at the counter, fellows, and I'll soon have you served."

"Well, well," said Zeph, staring around the place one way, then the other, and then repeating the performance. "This strikes me."

"Interesting to you, is it?" asked Ralph.

"It's wonderful. Fixed this up all alone out of odds and ends? I tell you, I'd like to be a partner in a business like this."

"Want a partner here, Joe?" called out Ralph to his friend in a jocular way.

"I want a helper," answered the cripple, busy among the shining cooking ware on a kitchen stove at one end of the restaurant.

"Mean that?" asked Zeph.

"I do. I have some new plans I want to carry out, and I need some one to attend to the place half of the time."

Again Zeph glanced all about the place.

"Say, it fascinates me," he observed to Ralph. "Upon my word, I believe I'll come to work here when I get through with this work for you."

"Tell you what," said Limpy Joe with a shrewd glance at Zeph, as he placed the smoking dishes before his customers. "I'll make it worth the while of an honest, active fellow to come in here with me. I have some grand ideas."

"You had some good ones when you fitted up the place," declared Zeph.

"You think it over. I like your looks," continued Joe. "I'm in earnest, and I might make it a partnership after a while."

The boys ate a hearty meal, and the young fireman paid for it.

"Business good, Joe?" he inquired, as they were about to leave.

"Famous. I've got some new customers, too. Don't know who they are."

"What's that?"

"I don't, for a fact."

"That sounds puzzling," observed Ralph.

"Well, it's considerable of a puzzle to me—all except the double pay I get," responded Joe. "For nearly a week I've had a funny order. One dark night some one pushed up a window here and threw in a card. It contained instructions and a ten-dollar bill."

"That's pretty mysterious," said the interested Zeph.

"The card told me that if I wanted to continue a good trade, I would say nothing about it, but every night at dark drive to a certain point in the timber yonder with a basket containing a good solid day's feed for half-a-dozen men."

"Well, well," murmured Zeph, while Ralph gave quite a start, but remained silent, though strictly attentive.

"Well, I have acted on orders given, and haven't said a word about it to anybody but you, Ralph. The reason I tell you is, because I think you are interested in some of the persons who are buying meals from me in this strange way. It's all right for me to speak out before your friend here?"

"Oh, certainly," assented Ralph.

"Well, Ike Slump is one of the party in the woods, and Mort Bemis is another."

"I guessed that the moment you began your story," said Ralph, "and I am looking for those very persons."

"I thought you would be interested. They are wanted for that attempted treasure-train robbery, aren't they?"

"Yes, and for a more recent occurrence," answered Ralph—"the looting of the Dover freight the other night."

"I never thought of that, though I should have done so," said Joe. "The way I know that Slump and Bemis are in the woods yonder, is that one night I had a breakdown, and was delayed a little, and saw them come for the food basket where I had left it."

Ralph's mind was soon made up. He told Joe all about their plans.

"You've got to help us out, Joe," he added.

"You mean take you up into the woods in the wagon to-night?"

"Yes."

"Say," said Joe, his shrewd eyes sparkling with excitement, "I'll do it in fine style. Ask no questions. I've got a plan. I'll have another breakdown, not a sham one, this time. I'll have you two well covered up in the wagon box, and you can lie there until some one comes after the basket."

"Good," approved Ralph, "you are a genuine friend, Joe."

Ralph and Zeph had to wait around the restaurant all the afternoon. There was only an occasional customer, and Joe had plenty of time to spare. He took a rare delight in showing his friends his treasures, as he called them.

About dusk Joe got the food supply ready for the party in the woods. He hitched up the horse to a wagon, arranged some blankets and hay in the bottom of the vehicle, so that his friends could hide themselves, and soon all was ready for the drive into the timber.

Ralph managed to look out as they proceeded into the woods. The wagon was driven about a mile. Then Joe got out and set the basket under a tree.

A little distance from it he got out again, took off a wheel, left it lying on the ground, unhitched the horse, and rode away on the back of the animal. The vehicle, to a casual observer, would suggest the appearance of a genuine breakdown.

"Now, Zeph," said Ralph as both arranged their coverings so they could view tree and basket clearly, "no rash moves."

"If anybody comes, what then?" inquired the farmer boy.

"We shall follow them, but with great caution. Keep close to me, so that I can give you special instructions, if it becomes necessary."

"Good," said Zeph. "That will be soon, for there they are!"

Two figures had appeared at the tree. One took up the basket, the other glanced around stealthily. Ralph recognized both of them, even in the dim twilight, at some distance away. One was Ike Slump, the other his old-time crony and accomplice, Mort Bemis.

CHAPTER VIII

THE HIDDEN PLUNDER

"That's the fellow who brought the package of silk to old Ames," whispered Zeph, staring hard from under covert at Slump.

"Yes, I recognize him," responded Ralph in quite as guarded a tone. "Quiet, now, Zeph."

Ike Slump and Mort Bemis continued to linger at the tree. They were looking at the wagon and beyond it.

"Say," spoke the former to his companion, "what's wrong?"

"How wrong?" inquired Mort.

"Why, some way our plans appear to have slipped a cog. There's the wagon broken down and the boy has gone with the horse. Two of our men were to stop him, you know, and keep him here while we used the wagon."

"Maybe they're behind time. What's the matter with our holding the boy till they come?"

"The very thing," responded Ike, and, leaving the basket where it was, he and Mort ran after Limpy Joe and the horse.

"Get out of here, quick," ordered Ralph to Zeph. "If we don't, we shall probably be carried into the camp of the enemy."

"Isn't that just exactly the place that you want to reach?" inquired the farmer boy coolly.

"Not in this way. Out with you, and into the bushes. Don't delay, Zeph, drop flat, some one else is coming."

It was a wonder they were not discovered, for almost immediately two men came running towards the spot. They were doubtless the persons Ike Slump had referred to, for they gave a series of signal whistles, responded to by their youthful accomplices, who, a minute later, came into view leading the horse of which Limpy Joe was astride.

"We were late," panted one of the men.

"Should think you were," retorted Ike Slump. "This boy nearly got away. Say, if you wasn't a cripple," he continued to the young restaurant keeper, "I'd give you something for whacking me with that crutch of yours."

"I'd whack you again, if it would do any good," said the plucky fellow. "You're a nice crowd, you are, bothering me this way after I've probably saved you from starvation the last week."

"That's all right, sonny," drawled out one of the men. "We paid you for what you've done for us, and we will pay you still better for simply coming to our camp and staying there a prisoner, until we use that rig of yours for a few hours."

"If you wanted to borrow the rig, why didn't you do so in a decent fashion?" demanded Joe indignantly.

"You keep quiet, now," advised the man who carried on the conversation. "We know our business. Here, Slump, you and Mort help get this wheel on the wagon and hitch up the horse."

They forced Joe into the wagon bottom and proceeded to get ready for a drive into the woods.

"Bet Joe is wondering how we came to get out of that wagon," observed Zeph to Ralph.

"Don't talk," said Ralph. "Now, when they start away, I will follow, you remain here."

"Right here?"

"Yes, so that I may find you when I come back, and so that you can follow the wagon when it comes out of the woods again if I am not on hand."

"You think they are going to move some of their plunder in the wagon?"

"Exactly," replied the young fireman.

"Well, so do I. They won't get far with it, though, if I am after them," boasted Zeph. "Wish I had a detective star and some weapons."

"The safest way to do is to follow them until they get near a town or settlement, and then go for assistance and arrest them," advised Ralph. "Now, then, Zeph, make no false moves."

"No, I will follow your orders strictly," pledged the farmer boy.

The basket was lifted into the wagon by Ike, who, with Mort, led the horse through the intricate timber and brushwood. Progress was difficult and they proceeded slowly. As soon as it was safe to do so, Ralph left Zeph. The two men had taken up the trail of the wagon, guarding its rear so that Joe could not escape.

Ralph kept sight of them for half-an-hour and was led deeper and deeper into the woods. These lined the railroad cut, and he wondered that the gang of robbers had dared to camp so near to the recent scene of their thieving operations.

At last the young fireman was following only two men, for he could no longer see the wagon.

"Perhaps they have left Ike and Bemis to go ahead with the wagon and they are reaching the camp by a short cut," reflected Ralph. "Why, no," he suddenly exclaimed, as the men turned aside to take a new path. "These are not the same men at all who were with the wagon. I am off the trail, I am following some one else."

Ralph made this discovery with some surprise. Certainly he had got mixed up in cautiously trailing the enemy at a distance. He wondered if the two men he was now following belonged to Ike Slump's crowd.

"I must assume they do," ruminated Ralph, "at least for the present. They are bound for some point in the woods, of course, and I shall soon know their destination."

The two men proceeded for over a mile. They commenced an ascent where the cliffs lining the railroad cut began. The place was thick with underbrush and quite rocky in places, wild and desolate in the extreme, and the path they pursued so tortuous and winding that Ralph at length lost sight of them.

"Where have they disappeared to?" he asked himself, bending his ear, keeping a sharp lookout, and with difficulty penetrating the worst jungle of bushes and stunted trees he had yet encountered. "I hear voices."

These guided Ralph, and he followed their indication. At last he came to a halt near an open space, where the men he was following had stopped.

"Here we are, Ames," were the first distinct words that Ralph heard spoken.

"Why, one of these men must be the farmer that Zeph worked for," decided Ralph.

"All right, you're safe enough up here. Got the plunder here, have you?" was asked.

"Yes. I will show you the exact spot, and you come here after we have got the bulk of the stuff to a new hiding place, take it as you can, dispose of it, and keep us in ready money until we feel safe to ship our goods to some distant city and realize on them."

"I'll do just that," was replied. "What are you leaving here for?"

"Adair, the road detective, is after us, we understand, and this is too dangerously near the railroad."

"That's so," replied the person Ralph supposed to be Ames. "All right, I'll not miss on my end of the case. Only, don't send any more packages of the silk to friends. The one Slump sent might have got you into trouble."

"I never knew he did it at the time," was responded. "I raised a big row when I found out. You see, Evans, the man he sent it to, is in with us in a way, and is a particular friend of Ike Slump, but it was a big risk to send him goods that might be traced right back to us. Safe hiding place, eh?"

The speaker had proceeded to some bushes guarding the entrance to a cave-like depression in the dirt, gravel and rocks. He re-appeared with some packages for his companion. Then both went away from the spot.

"Why," said Ralph, with considerable satisfaction, "this is the hiding place of the plunder. I am in possession, and what am I going to do about it?"

The discovery had come about so easily that the young fireman could scarcely plan out a next intelligent move all in a moment.

"Ames is an accomplice of the thieves," he decided, "who are going to use Joe's wagon to remove the bulk of this plunder. They will soon be here. What had I better do—what can I do?"

Ralph went in among the bushes as the men had done. He took a glance at a great heap of packages lying in a depression in the rocks. Then he advanced a few steps towards the edge of the cliff.

Ralph looked down fully two hundred feet into the railroad cut. This was almost the spot where the landslide had stopped the Dover night freight. The main tracks were clear now, but on a gravel pit siding were several cars.

"Why," exclaimed Ralph suddenly, "if I only have the time to do it in, I have got the whole affair right in my own hands."

A plan to deprive the railroad thieves of their booty had come into the mind of the young fireman. Ralph filled his arms with the packages of silk, advanced to the edge of the cliff, threw them over, and continued his operation until he had removed the last parcel from its hiding place.

"Something more to do yet," he told himself, when this task was completed. "When the thieves discover that their plunder is gone, they may surmise that it disappeared this way. Can I make a safe descent?"

Ralph had a hard time getting down into the railroad cut. Once there, he hastily threw the silk packages into a half-filled gravel car, with a shovel covered them all over with sand and gravel, and then started on a run for Brocton.

CHAPTER IX

A SUSPICIOUS PROCEEDING

"Mr. Griscom, this is life!"

Ralph Fairbanks spoke with all the ardor of a lively, ambitious boy in love with the work in hand. He sat in the cab of the locomotive that drew the Limited Mail, and he almost felt as if he owned the splendid engine, the finest in the service of the Great Northern.

Two weeks had passed by since the young fireman had baffled the railroad thieves. Ralph had made brief work of his special duty for Adair, the road detective, and there had come to him a reward for doing his duty that was beyond his fondest expectations. This was a promotion that most beginners in his line would not have earned in any such brief space of time. The recovery of the stolen silk, however, had made Bob Adair a better friend than ever. The road detective had influence, and Ralph was promoted to the proud position of fireman of the Limited Mail.

This was his first trip in the passenger service, and naturally Ralph was anxious and excited. Griscom had been made engineer, his eyes having mended, and Ralph was very glad that the veteran railroader would continue as his partner.

Regarding the silk robbery, that was now ancient history, but for several days the occurrence had been one of interest all along the line. Adair had made public the circumstances of the case, and Ralph became quite a hero.

The night he had managed to get the plunder into the gravel car he had instantly secured assistance at Brocton. The valuable goods were guarded all night, and a party of men made a search for the thieves, but they had taken the alarm and had escaped.

Zeph Dallas had gone back to Millville with Limpy Joe, and went to work there. A further search was made for Ike Slump, Mort Bemis and their accomplices, but they could not be found. Jim Evans had been discharged from the railroad service. Nothing more was heard of Gasper Farrington, and it seemed to Ralph as if at last his enemies had been fully routed and there was nothing but a clear track ahead.

"It feels as if I was beginning life all over again," Ralph had told his mother that morning. "Fireman of the Limited Mail—just think of it, mother! one of the best positions on the road."

Ralph decided that the position demanded very honorable treatment, and he looked neat and quite dressed up, even in his working clothes, as he now sat in the engine cab.

Griscom proceeded to give him lots of suggestions and information regarding his new duties.

There had been a change in the old time schedule of the Limited Mail. Originally it had started from the city terminus in the early morning. Now the run was reversed, and the train left Stanley Junction at 10:15 A.M.

Ralph proceeded to get everything in order for the prospective run, but everything was so handy, it was a pleasure to contemplate his duties.

Just before train time a boy came running up to the engine. He was an old schoolmate and a neighbor.

"Ralph! Ralph!" he called breathlessly to the young fireman. "Your mother sent me with a letter that she got at the post-office."

"For me? Thank you, Ned," said Ralph.

He glanced at the address. The handwriting was unfamiliar. There was no time left to inspect the enclosure, so Ralph slipped the letter in his pocket and proceeded to attend to the fire.

He quite forgot the letter after that, finding the duties of a first-class fireman to be extremely arduous. There was plenty of coal to shovel, and he was pretty well tired out when they reached the city terminus.

"There, lad," said Griscom proudly, as they steamed into the depot on time to a second. "This makes me feel like old times once more."

There was a wait of four hours in the city, during which period the train hands were at liberty to spend their time as they chose. Griscom took Ralph to a neat little hotel, where they had a meal and the privileges of a reading room. It was there that Ralph suddenly remembered the letter sent to him that morning by his mother.

As he opened it he was somewhat puzzled, for the signature was strange to him. The missive stated that the writer "was acting for a former resident of Stanley Junction who wished to settle up certain obligations, if a satisfactory arrangement could be made." Further the writer, as agent of the party in question, would meet Ralph at a certain hotel at a certain time and impart to him his instructions.

The young fireman was about to consult Griscom as to this mysterious missive, but found the old engineer engaged in conversation with some fellow railroaders, and, leaving the place, he proceeded to the hotel named in the letter.

He was an hour ahead of the time appointed in the communication and waited patiently for developments, thinking a good deal and wondering what would come of the affair.

Finally a man came into the place, acting as if he was looking for somebody. He was an under-sized person with a mean and crafty face. He glanced at Ralph, hesitated somewhat, and then advanced towards him.

"Is your name Fairbanks?" he questioned.

"Yes," answered Ralph promptly.

"Wrote you a letter."

"I received one, yes," said Ralph. "May I ask its meaning?"

"Well, there is nothing gained by beating about the bush. I represent, as an attorney, Mr. Gasper Farrington."

"I thought that when I read your letter," said Ralph.

"Then we understand each other," pursued the attorney. "Now then, see here, Farrington wants to do the square thing by you."

"He ought to," answered Ralph. "He owes us twenty thousand dollars and he has got to pay it."

"Oh, yes, you can undoubtedly collect it in time," admitted the man.

"But why all this mystery?" asked Ralph abruptly. "In an important matter like this, it appears to me some regular attorney might consult our attorneys at Stanley Junction."

"Farrington won't do that. He don't feel the kindest in the world towards your people. Here is his simple proposition: This affair is to be settled up quietly between the parties directly interested. I am to give you certain papers for your mother to sign. You get them attended to. You will be later advised where and when to deliver them and get your money."

"Twenty thousand dollars?" said Ralph.

"Yes."

Ralph did not like the looks of things, but he kept his own counsel, and simply said:

"Very well, give me the documents you speak of and I will act upon them as my mother decides."

"And keep the business strictly to yourselves."

This looked reasonable to Ralph. He knew that Farrington felt deeply the disgrace already attached to his name for past misdeeds of which he had been guilty.

"We have no desire to humiliate Mr. Farrington any further," he said. "We simply insist upon our rights. This strikes me as a mysterious and uncalled-for method of settling up a claim purely business-like in its character."

"That is the way of old Farrington, you know," suggested the man, with a coarse laugh.

"Yes, he seems to be given to dark ways," said Ralph.

"Then it is all arranged?" questioned the "lawyer" eagerly.

"So far as it can be arranged for the time being."

"Very well, you shall hear from us in a few days."

Ralph left the hotel with one fixed conviction in his mind—that old Gasper Farrington was up to some new scheme and that it would be wise to look out for him.

CHAPTER X

THE SPECIAL

Within a week the young fireman of the Limited Mail was in full swing as a trusted and valued employe of the Great Northern. Engineer Griscom had got the time schedule down to a system of which he was proud. They made successful runs without a break or accident, and Ralph loved the life for its variety, experience and promise of sure promotion.

The documents given to him for his mother by the agent of Gasper Farrington in the city were apparently all regular and business-like. They covered receipt for twenty thousand dollars, designating certain numbered bonds indicated, but one phrase which exonerated the village magnate from blame or crooked dealing in the affair Ralph did not at all like. He believed that there was some specious scheme under this matter and he awaited developments.

One blustering night he and Griscom had just run the engine into the roundhouse, when Tim Forgan, the foreman, came hastening towards them, a paper fluttering in his hand and accompanied by a young fellow about twenty years of age. The latter was handsome and manly-looking, very well dressed, and Ralph liked him on sight.

"The very men," spoke Forgan, showing an unusual excitement of manner. "Griscom, Fairbanks, let me introduce you to Mr. Trevor."

Engineer and fireman bowed, but the young man insisted on shaking hands cordially with his new acquaintances.

"Glad to meet you, gentlemen," he said briskly. "I have heard nothing but regrets as to your absence and praises for your ability in the railroad line from Forgan here. Tell your story, Mr. Forgan. You know time is money to me, just at present," and the speaker consulted an elegant timepiece in a hurried, anxious way.

"Why, it's just this," said Forgan. "Mr. Trevor, who is a nephew of the president of the road, came to me with a telegram directing us to send him through to the city on the quickest time on record."

"A special, eh?" said Griscom, eyeing the young man speculatively.

"About that, only there is no time to waste in making up a train, and he inclines to riding on the locomotive. The train dispatcher will give clear tracks to terminus. We were just picking out an engine when you arrived. How is it, Griscom?"

"You mean, will we undertake the job?" inquired the veteran engineer in his practical, matter-of-fact way.

"Exactly," nodded Trevor eagerly.

"After a hard double run?" insinuated Griscom.

"That's so; it isn't right to ask them, Forgan. Give me some other engine."

"Won't you wait till I answer?" demanded Griscom. "Yes, we will, and glad to show you the courtesy. Is that right, Fairbanks?"

"Certainly," replied Ralph. "Is it a matter of a great deal of urgency, Mr. Trevor?"

"Particularly so. I have come five hundred miles on other roads on specials. I must connect with a train in the city at a certain time, or I miss Europe and important business."

Old Griscom took out his greasy, well-worn train schedule. He looked it over and pointing to the regular time made, said:

"We can discount that exactly seventy-two minutes."

"And that will bring me to terminus exactly on time," said the young man brightly. "Do it, my friends, and you shall have a hundred dollars between you."

"That isn't at all necessary"—began Griscom.

"I beg pardon, but in this case it is," broke in Trevor. "It's all arranged. Thanks. I will put on a rain coat, and if you will stow me in some corner of the tender I shall enjoy the run."

Forgan bustled about. Through the call boy of the roundhouse Ralph sent word to his mother of the extra trip. Then he worked like a beaver on the locomotive. Trevor watched him in a pleased and admiring way.

They ran the locomotive out on the turn table. Griscom consulted his watch, talked a few moments with Forgan, and said to Ralph:

"Tracks clear in twelve minutes, lad. Just time enough to get a bite at the nearest restaurant."

When they returned, Trevor stood near the engine glancing all around him in a very animated way.

"Looking for Forgan?" inquired the old engineer.

"Oh, no. I was wondering where a fellow disappeared to who was hanging around the tender a few minutes ago. He and a companion have been following me ever since I arrived."

"Then they have given up the job," observed Griscom, glancing keenly about. "Why should they follow you, Mr. Trevor?"

"That I cannot tell. Probably thought I looked prosperous, and were bent on waylaying me. Anyhow, they kept close to me down the tracks from the depot. Ready?"

"In precisely one minute. There is the Dover Accommodation now," announced the engineer, as a headlight came around a curve. "All right. We'll have to coal up at the limits. Then we will make you a comfortable seat, Mr. Trevor."

"Don't you give yourselves any concern about me," replied Trevor. "I am used to railroad life."

They coaled up at the limits, but did not stop for water, the tank being three-quarters full. Ralph made tests of air valve and water pump, shook down the furnace, and the locomotive quivered under high-steam pressure as they started on their special run.

A flagman shouted something at them as they passed a switch.

"What was he saying?" inquired Griscom.

"I couldn't hear him," said Ralph.

"Thought he pointed at the engine—at the cow-catcher," remarked Trevor.

"Everything all right there," assured Ralph, and in the brisk action of the hour the circumstance was forgotten.

Twenty, thirty, forty miles made, and as they slowed down Griscom turned to Trevor, a proud glitter in his eye.

"How is that, sir?" he inquired.

"Famous!" cried the young man cheerily. "Badly shaken up, and this seat up here is rather bumpy, but I enjoy it, just the same. Going to stop?"

"Yes, crossing. Only for half-a-minute, though."

The engine halted on regular signal. Griscom got down and ran about a bit, explaining that he was subject to cramps when seated long in one position. Two men came up to the locomotive.

"Give us a lift?" demanded one of them.

"Couldn't do it, partner," responded Ralph. "Under special orders."

"Plenty of room up there on the tender."

"Not for you," answered the young fireman.

Both men regarded Trevor very keenly. Then they disappeared in the darkness. Ralph got the signal from the crossing's switch tower to go ahead.

"Mr. Griscom," he called out from his window.

"Why, where is he?—I don't see him," said Trevor in surprise. "I saw him out there not a minute ago."

Ralph jumped to the ground in amazement. Nowhere in sight was Griscom; nowhere within hearing either, it seemed. Like the two rough fellows who had just approached the engine, Griscom has disappeared.

"Why, this is mysterious," declared the young fireman in an anxious tone of concern. "Where can he have disappeared to?"

"I don't like the looks of things," spoke Trevor. "Something is wrong, Fairbanks," he continued. "Look ahead there—I just saw a man on the cowcatcher."

Now Ralph was more than mystified, he was alarmed. He seized a rod and jumped again to the ground. Sure enough, on the cowcatcher sat a man, huddled up comfortably.

"Who are you?" demanded Ralph, keeping his distance and eyeing the intruder suspiciously.

"Call me a tramp, if you like," laughed the fellow.

"You must get off of that cowcatcher."

"Who says so?"

"I do—against the rules. Come, move on."

"You try to put me off, youngster," drawled the fellow, with an ugly look in his eyes, "and I'll use this," and he drew a revolver from his pocket. "I want a free ride, and I intend to have it."

"Will you make me stop at the tower to get you put off?" threatened Ralph.

"You won't. There's no one there but the towerman, and he can't leave duty, and you won't stop because you're on a fast run. Take it easy, sonny. I don't weigh much, and I won't hurt your old locomotive."

Ralph could do nothing better than submit to the imposition for the time being. He returned to the cab. His face was quite anxious. He called again to Griscom.

"I can't understand it," he said. "What can have befallen him? Keep a close watch here for a few minutes, will you?" he asked of his passenger.

Ralph took a lantern and ran down the tracks, flashed the light across the empty freights lining the tracks, and returned to the locomotive more anxious than ever.

"I can't think what to do, Mr. Trevor," he said.

The young man consulted his watch nervously.

"Tell you, Fairbanks, we mustn't lose time. You can't find your partner. Run to the tower and have the man there telegraph the circumstances and get someone to look for Griscom. We will have to run on without him."

"Without Griscom!" cried Ralph. "Why, we cannot possibly secure a substitute this side of Dover."

"Don't need one—you know how to run an engine, don't you?"

"In a fashion, probably, but I am worried about Mr. Griscom."

"The towerman can attend to that. I don't want to appear selfish, Fairbanks, but you must get this special through on time or get to some point where we can find another engineer."

"I don't like it," said Ralph. "Without a fireman, too."

"I'll attend to that department," said Trevor, briskly throwing off his coat. "Now then, the tower, your word to the operator there, and make up for lost time, Fairbanks, if you want to earn that hundred dollars."

CHAPTER XI

KIDNAPPED

Ralph climbed to the engineer's seat with many misgivings and very anxious concerning his missing partner. He knew how to run an engine, for the young fireman had watched Griscom at his duties, had studied every separate piece of machinery thoroughly, and more than once had relieved the veteran engineer for brief periods of time between stations.

"That was all well enough on a regular run," thought Ralph, "but a special is a different thing."

Then, coming to the switch tower, he called up to the operator there, who was at the open window. He explained hurriedly about the disappearance of Griscom. He also asked the towerman to telegraph ahead to Dover for a substitute engineer. The operator said he would have some men come down from the first station back on the route on a handcar to search for the missing rail-roader.

"Man on your cowcatcher there," he called down as Ralph started up the engine.

"No time to bother with him now. Let him ride to Dover, if he wants to," advised Trevor. "Now, Fairbanks, you to the throttle, me to the furnace. Just give me a word of direction when I need it, won't you?"

But for his anxiety concerning his missing partner, the young fireman would have enjoyed the run of the next two hours immensely. There was a clear track—he had only to look out for signals. He was entirely familiar with the route, and Trevor proved a capable, practical assistant.

"Don't look much like the man who left a palace car to step into a locomotive at Stanley Junction, eh?" laughed the young man, reeking with perspiration, and greasy and grimed. "How do I do—all right?"

"You must have had experience in the fireman line," submitted Ralph.

"Why, yes," acknowledged Trevor. "My uncle made me work in a roundhouse for a year. Once I believe I could run an engine, but I've forgotten a good deal. Fairbanks, look ahead!"

There was no occasion for the warning. Already the young fireman had discovered what his companion announced. As the locomotive glided around a sharp curve a great glare confronted them.

Not two hundred yards ahead was a mass of flames shooting skywards. The bridge crossing a creek that was located at this part of the route was on fire.

Ralph started to slow down. Then, discerning the impossibility of doing so this side of the burning structure, he set full speed.

"It's make or break," he said, in a kind of gasp.

"Put her through—take the risk," ordered Trevor sharply.

Swish! crackle! crash!—it was an eventful moment in the career of the young fireman. There was a blinding glow, a rain of fire swayed through the locomotive cab, then, just as they cleared the bridge, the structure went down to midstream.

"We must get this news to Dover quick," said Ralph, applying himself anew to lever and throttle. "We have ten minutes to make up then."

Clink!—snap!—a terrific jar shook the locomotive. Contrary to signal given at the nearest switch ahead, the engine veered to a siding.

"What does this mean?" demanded Trevor sharply.

"Mischief—malice, perhaps," said Ralph quickly. "Freights ahead—we shall have to stop."

"Don't do it," directed Trevor. "Drive into them and push them ahead to the main line again. I'll stand all damage."

"They are empties, I noticed them on the afternoon run," said the young fireman. "Mr. Trevor, all this complication, all these happenings are suspicious. We will have to slow down to the freights."

"Slow down entirely," growled a sudden voice. "Do it, or I'll have it done by my partner, who is aboard all right."

Both Ralph and Trevor turned sharply. Standing on the coal of the tender was a man. He was dripping with water, and in one hand held a revolver.

"No delay, Fairbanks," he cautioned sternly. "We've taken too much trouble to miss this last chance to get you and your passenger."

Ralph stopped the engine. Then calmly, but with a certain sense of peril and defeat, he faced the man.

"Where did you come from?" demanded Trevor in amazement.

"Only from inside the water tank," responded the stranger coolly. "Been there since we left Stanley Junction."

"Why, you are one of the fellows who were following me at the depot!" cried Trevor.

"Correct, boss," chuckled the stranger. "Here's my partner," he announced, as the man Ralph had discovered on the cowcatcher appeared at the side of the cab. "We'll relieve you two now," continued the speaker to Ralph and Trevor. "Move back on that coal. We'll try a bit of engineering ourselves."

"See here, my man," called out Trevor sharply. "What is the object of all this?"

"Object?" grinned the man. "You'll know later. Important, for it took four men on the route, lots of inquiring before you came to Stanley Junction, two of us here now, others waiting for us somewhere else, to get you dead right."

"Me!" exclaimed Trevor in amazement. "You mean me?"

"Nobody else."

"Why, how are you interested in me?"

"You'll know soon."

"But—"

"Stand back, do as we say, or we'll use force," declared the speaker gruffly.

His companion guarded Ralph and Trevor while he took the engineer's seat. He reversed the engine, ran back to the main tracks, from there, first setting a switch, onto a spur, and, after following this for nearly a mile, shut off steam and the locomotive came to a stop.

Then the fellow applied a whistle to his lips. Several men approached the engine. He consulted with them, and came back to Ralph carrying a piece of rope.

"Fairbanks," he said, "we'll have to tie you for safe keeping for a while."

"Won't you explain this?" inquired Trevor, in a troubled way. "See here, men, I am due in the city. I will pay you handsomely to let us proceed on our trip."

"How much?" inquired the man who had acted as engineer.

"I have several hundred dollars with me."

"Not enough," retorted the man. "We want several thousand, seeing you are worth it."

"I haven't a thousand dollars in the world," declared Trevor.

"You are worth twenty thousand," insisted the man confidently. "We'll prove it to you a little later. Here," to his companion, "tie Fairbanks, leave the letter with him, and let us get out of this before anybody is missed."

"One word," said Ralph. "Are you people responsible for the disappearance of Mr. Griscom?"

"Perhaps," said the man. "He's all safe and sound—only out of the way of mischief for a spell. One other word, Fairbanks, we didn't fire the bridge."

Trevor looked the picture of distress and uncertainty as he was forced from the locomotive cab.

47

"You people will regret this high-handed outrage," he cried. "My uncle is president of the Great Northern."

"That is just exactly why you are worth twenty thousand dollars," coolly announced the man who had acted as engineer. "Plain and square, gentlemen, kindly call this a bit of kidnapping scientifically worked at some care and expense. You come with us. Fairbanks will do the rest. Got him tied up?" to his companion. "All right, now put the letter in his pocket."

And, leaving the young fireman bound and helpless on the floor of the cab, the men with Trevor left the scene.

CHAPTER XII

THE RAILROAD PRESIDENT

The young fireman had a good deal to think of as he lay in the locomotive cab, unable to help himself in any way. All the smooth sailing of the past week was remembered in strong contrast to the anxieties of the present moment.

Ralph had not recognized any of the crowd who had appeared about the engine during the evening. The leader, however, seemed to know his name. This inclined Ralph to the belief that some one of the party did know him, and naturally he thought of Ike Slump and his associates.

"They are desperate men, whoever they are," he decided, "and they must have planned out this scheme to perfection to keep track of Mr. Trevor and follow us up along the line. That man in the water tank is a daring fellow. He must have had a pleasant time in there. It was an original move, anyhow."

It was in vain that Ralph endeavored to release himself. He was stoutly tied. All he could do was to wriggle about and wonder how soon he would be set free by his captors or discovered by others.

It must have been fully three hours before there was any break in the monotony of his situation. Ralph heard some one whistling a tune and approaching rapidly. Soon a man appeared on the cab step, looked Ralph over coolly, and observed:

"Tired of waiting for me, kid?"

"Naturally," responded Ralph. "Are you going to set me free?"

"That's the orders, seeing that our party is safe at a distance. Got enough steam on to run the engine?"

"Yes," replied Ralph. "There was full pressure when you people stopped us, and the steam lasts about six hours."

"All right. You will have a great story to tell the railroad folks, eh? Don't forget the letter we put in your pocket. There you are. Now then, go about your business and don't say we did not treat you like a gentleman. Oh—ooh! What's this?"

The man had cut the ropes that held Ralph captive, and carelessly swung to the step. In a flash the young fireman was on his mettle. Springing to his feet, Ralph snatched at a hooked rod. Reaching out, he caught the man by the coat collar and pulled him back flat across the cab floor where he had just lain.

"You lie still, or I shall use harsh measures," declared Ralph, springing upon his captive and menacing him with the rod. "Hold up your hands, folded, and let me tie you."

"Well, I guess not!"

"Yes, you shall!" cried Ralph.

In a second the situation changed. The man was much stronger than his opponent. He managed to throw Ralph off, and got to his knees. The young fireman decided, as the fellow reached for a weapon, to strike out with the iron rod. It landed heavily on the man's temple, and he fell back senseless on the coal of the tender with a groan.

Ralph securely tied his captive. Then he reversed the lever and opened the throttle. In a minute he was speeding back over the spur the way the locomotive had come four hours previous.

"We have one of the kidnappers, at least," he said with satisfaction. "Ah, there is some one at the bridge," he added, as he ran down the main tracks.

Signals of danger were set on both sides of the creek, and Ralph could make out men in the distance moving about. He was soon on the scene.

A track-walker had discovered the burning bridge and had summoned assistance.

There was only one thing to do with the locomotive, to run on to Dover, and this Ralph did at once. He reported the occurrences of the evening to the assistant superintendent, whom he found getting a wrecking crew together.

"Well, this is a serious and amazing piece of business," commented that official. "Here, men," he called to his assistants on the wrecking car, "fetch this fellow into the shanty yonder."

The man Ralph had knocked down in the locomotive cab had recovered consciousness. He was brought into the shanty and questioned, but was sullen and silent.

"Won't tell anything, eh?" said the assistant superintendent.

"The letter says all there is to say," remarked the captive coolly, "but that twenty thousand dollars will never find young Trevor if you keep me a prisoner."

"A prisoner safe and tight you shall be," declared the railroad official with determination. "Take him to the town jail, men," he added. "I must wire for the president of the road at once, and to Adair at Stanley Junction. What's your plan, Fairbanks?" he asked of Ralph.

"I hardly know," responded the young fireman. "I don't see that I can be of any assistance here."

The letter the kidnappers had left with Ralph was terse and clear as to its directions. The writer demanded twenty thousand dollars for the return of young Trevor, and indicated how his friends might get in correspondence with his captors through an advertisement in the city newspapers.

"The wrecking car is going to the bridge, Fairbanks," said the official. "You can cross the creek some way and use a handcar, if they have one. Tell the men there I say so. As to your prisoner, I will see that he is taken care of."

It was just daylight when Ralph reached the switch tower where Griscom had disappeared. The towerman had just been relieved from duty, and met Ralph with eager welcome as he was approaching the place.

"Glad to see you," he said. "We just found Griscom."

"Where is he?" inquired Ralph quickly.

"In the tower, all safe and comfortable now, but he had a hard time of it lying all night in a freight car, gagged and tied. He is fighting mad, don't understand the affair, and worried to death about you."

"Oh, I am all right," said Ralph.

"I see you are. But what has happened, anyhow? You'll want to tell Griscom, won't you? Well, I'll go back with you to hear your story, too."

It was an interesting scene, the meeting of the engineer and the young fireman. Griscom fretted and fumed over the mishaps to his pet locomotive. He was furious at the gang who had worked out such mischief.

"I'll wire my resignation when we reach Stanley Junction," he declared. "I'll do no more railroad work until I find those scoundrels and rescue young Trevor."

"Don't be rash, Mr. Griscom," advised Ralph. "The railroad detective force will soon be on the trail. The nephew of a railroad president doesn't disappear in this fashion every day in the year."

When they got back to Stanley Junction they were interviewed at once by Bob Adair. Both were worn out with double duty and got to bed as quickly as possible.

Ralph reported at the roundhouse late in the afternoon, but learned that there would be no through trains out until a temporary bridge was erected over the creek near Dover.

He returned to the house, and was pleased with the thought of having a social evening at home and a good night's rest.

It was shortly after dark, and Ralph was reading a book in the cozy sitting room of the home cottage, when the door bell rang.

The young fireman answered the summons. A stranger stood at the threshold. He was a dignified, well-dressed gentleman, but seemed to be laboring under some severe mental strain, for he acted nervous and agitated.

"Mr. Fairbanks—Ralph Fairbanks?" he inquired in a tone of voice that quivered slightly.

"Yes," replied the young fireman.

"I am very anxious to have a talk with you," said the stranger hurriedly. "I have been down the line, and have just arrived at Stanley Junction. My name is Grant, Robert Grant, and I am the president of the Great Northern Railroad."

"Come in, sir," said Ralph cordially, deeply impressed with welcoming so important a visitor, but maintaining his usual manly pose. He showed the official into the house and introduced him to his mother.

Mr. Grant was soon in the midst of his story. He had been for many hours at Dover trying to discover a trace of his missing nephew, and had signally failed.

"Mr. Adair, the road detective, advised me to see you," said Mr. Grant, "for you saw the men who captured my nephew. Would you know them again?"

"Some of them," responded Ralph.

"Very well, then. I ask you as a special favor to return with me to Dover and assist me in my task."

"I will do so gladly," said Ralph.

One hour later a special conveyed the president of the Great Northern and Ralph Fairbanks down the line to Dover.

CHAPTER XIII

THE SHORT LINE RAILWAY

Ralph attracted a good deal of attention when he arrived at Dover, and fully realized the honor of being treated as a companion by the president of the great railroad of which he was an employe. Mr. Grant was pleasant and friendly. He learned Ralph's story, and discussed railroad experience in a way that was enlightening and encouraging to the young fireman.

"About these kidnappers," he said, "I will never give them a dollar, but I will spend all I have to rescue my nephew. It is needless to say that you shall be richly rewarded if you assist me successfully."

"I will do my best, sir," pledged Ralph.

At Dover they were met by Adair. They went into the depot and sat down on a bench in a remote corner.

"I have not discovered the kidnappers nor the faintest clew to them, Mr. Grant," said Adair.

The railroad president sighed deeply. He showed in his face and manner the care and anxiety he was suffering.

"Can you suggest anything, Fairbanks?" continued Adair. "You know the district fairly well. What is your idea about these men?"

Ralph astonished his companions by suddenly arising to his feet and hurrying towards a boy who had just entered the depot and had taken up a pen and a telegraph pad on the counter outside the ticket office.

It was Van Sherwin, the old-time friend of Ralph, and pleasure at recognizing him had caused the young fireman to act on an impulse.

"Why, Van!" he cried, "I am glad to see you."

"Eh?" spoke the other. "Ralph! well, the gladness is mutual," and the pair shook hands cordially.

"What brought you here?" asked Ralph.

"Came down from headquarters in the timber on important business," replied Van. "Just sending a telegram."

"Why!" almost shouted Ralph, glancing at the blank upon which his friend had just written a name, "to Mr. Grant, to the president of the Great Northern!"

"Yes," answered Van. "Does that startle you?"

"It does. What are you wiring him for?"

"About his nephew, Dudley Trevor."

Ralph was fairly taken off his feet, as the saying goes. He grasped Van's arm excitedly.

"See here, Van Sherwin," he cried. "What do you know of Mr. Trevor?"

"Only that he is at our headquarters with a broken arm, and he sent me here to wire his uncle the fact."

Ralph was delighted. He could scarcely credit the glad news. He led Van up to the railroad president and the road detective with the words:

"Gentlemen, I am very happy to tell you that Mr. Trevor is in safe hands, and my friend here will explain. Van Sherwin, this is Mr. Grant, the president of the Great Northern."

Van nodded in his crisp, off-hand way to Adair, whom he knew, and took off his cap to his dignified companion.

His story was to his auditors most remarkable and exciting, but to Van only the narration of a perfectly natural occurrence. Early that morning there had come into "headquarters," as Van termed it, a young man in an almost exhausted condition. His attire was all torn with brambles and bushes and one arm was broken.

"He told us his name, and said that he had escaped from kidnappers. Mr. Gibson attended to his arm, and sent me to Dover here to telegraph to you, sir," explained Van to the railroad president.

Mr. Grant was so glad and excited he could not sit still.

"Take me to him at once!" he cried. "My dear lad, you have brought happy news to me."

"I don't know about going to see him," said Van. "It is over twenty miles away in the woods."

"Allow me to explain, Mr. Grant," said Adair. "Between here and Wilmer is a wild, wooded stretch of land known as The Barrens."

"I know of it," nodded Mr. Grant. "The Great Northern once surveyed two miles into the section, but abandoned the route as impracticable. There are only about twenty houses in the district, and the difficulties of clearing and grading were discouraging."

"Well," said Adair, "it appears that a man named Farwell Gibson secured a charter to build a short line through The Barrens from Wilmer across the desolate tract to connect with the Midland Central."

"I heard of that, too," nodded the railroad president.

"This Gibson is an odd genius. He has been working for two years on his scheme, terming the road the Dover & Springfield Short Line. Just half way

54

across The Barrens he has a house, which he calls 'headquarters.' He is an erratic hermit, and adopted this boy here, Van Sherwin, who has been helping him. Every day, the law requires, he must do some grading work on the prospective railroad line. This he has done, and you would be surprised to know the progress they have made."

"Especially lately," said Van, with sparkling eyes. "Even you, Ralph, would be astonished. Mrs. Gibson got some money recently—five thousand dollars from old Gasper Farrington—and we have hired a lot of men. Oh, that railroad is going through, and don't you forget it."

"We realized our mistake after this Gibson got hold of the franchise," said Mr. Grant. "Once the road is built, it practically dominates passenger and freight business north and south."

"That is right," said Van, "for it becomes a bee-line, saving twenty to thirty miles distance, besides opening up a new district. Well, sir, your nephew is now at our headquarters. To reach the place you will have to get a very heavy wagon and go pretty slow and sure, for there are no roads."

"I must go at all hazards," cried the railroad president insistently, "and you, my friends, must accompany me," he added to Adair and Ralph. "Why, those villains from whom my nephew escaped may undertake to recapture him."

A little later the party, in charge of a sturdy fellow driving a strong team of horses attached to a heavy wagon, started out under the direction of Van Sherwin.

The district was a wild jungle, interspersed with sweeps of hill and dales, and numerous creeks. Finally they reached a hill surmounted by a dense grove of trees. A road led up here to a rambling log house.

Here and on the other side of the hill a ten-foot avenue was visible, neat and clean. The brush had been cleared away, the ground leveled, here and there some rudely cut ties set in place, and for an extended stretch there was a presentable graded roadbed.

As they drove up to the cabin the railroad president almost forgot his nephew from interest in his surroundings. Across the front of the building was a sign reading: "Headquarters of the Dover & Springfield Short Line Railroad." To the south there was a singular sight presented. Some twenty men and boys were working on a roadbed, which had been cut for over two miles. A telegraph wire ran from the building over the tops of trees, and Ralph was fairly astonished at the progress made since he had first visited Farwell Gibson in this place.

"Come in," said Van, as Mr. Grant alighted from the wagon.

"Well, this is decidedly a railroady place," observed the president of the Great Northern with a faint smile.

One half of the rambling place was a depot and railway offices combined. There were benches for passengers. In one corner was a partitioned off space, labeled: "President's Office." On the wall hung a bunch of blank baggage checks, and there was a chart of a zigzag railway line, indicating bridges, water tanks and switch towers.

"Mr. Gibson," called out Van to a man seated at a desk, "this is Mr. Grant, the president of the Great Northern."

"Eh? what! My dear sir, I am glad to see you," said the eccentric hermit. "You came about your nephew, I presume? Take the gentleman to his room, Van," directed Farwell. "I am something of a doctor and he is resting quite comfortably."

Mr. Gibson greeted Ralph very cordially. When Van returned, he insisted on the young fireman inspecting the work on the railroad.

"Does that look like business?" he inquired, as they proceeded down the roadbed. "We have ten men and eight boys working for us."

"Eight boys—where did they come from?" inquired Ralph.

"An orphan asylum burned down and we engaged to care for them," replied Van.

"But what are they doing in those trees?"

"Stringing a telegraph wire. We expect within a month to have the telegraph through to Springfield, and later to Dover."

"Why, Van," said Ralph, "it seems incredible, the progress you have made."

"That five thousand dollars we made old Farrington pay Mrs. Gibson was a great help," replied Van. "We have quite a construction crew here now. I help Mrs. Gibson do the cooking, and we get on famously."

Mr. Grant was with his nephew for over an hour. Then Ralph was sent for, and Trevor welcomed him with a glad smile. The young man described how he had been taken to a lonely building in the woods, how he had escaped from his enemies, breaking his arm in a runaway flight, and telling Ralph that he intended to remain where he was for a month, to which his uncle had agreed.

"Confidentially, Fairbanks," he said, "I have taken a great interest in this Short Cut Railroad scheme, and as soon as I am well I am coming to see you at Stanley Junction."

"Regarding this railroad?" inquired Ralph.

"Exactly," responded Trevor. "I see a great future in it. I shall not go to Europe. There is a practical business chance here, and I intend to help Mr. Gibson get the enterprise through."

"It will take a lot of money," suggested Ralph.

"Yes," assented Trevor, "and I know how to raise it. In fact, I have almost agreed to market one hundred thousand dollars' worth of bonds of the Dover & Springfield Short Line Railroad, and I want you to help me do it."

CHAPTER XIV

A RAILROAD STRIKE

"It's a bad outlook, lad," said old John Griscom.

The veteran engineer was serious and anxious as he pronounced the words. He and Ralph were proceeding down the tracks beyond the round-house, just returned from their regular run from the city.

"It's a strike, is it?" inquired Ralph.

"Worse than a strike," replied Griscom. "The railroad men's union is in a squabble among themselves and a fight is on. That means trouble and damage all around."

It was two weeks after the kidnapping of young Trevor, and affairs had subsided to regular routine for the engineer and fireman of the Limited Mail. The president of the Great Northern had sent a check for one hundred dollars to Ralph, which he divided with Griscom, both making up twenty-five dollars for Van Sherwin. From the actions of their superiors they knew that their being in close touch with Mr. Grant had helped them considerably, and both felt secure and contented in their positions, when a new disturbing element appeared.

For several days there had been trouble on both the Great Northern and the Midland Central. As Ralph understood it, the discharge of an irresponsible engineer on the latter line of railroad had led to a demand for his reinstatement. This the railway officials refused. A strike was at once ordered.

Two days later a man named Delmay, a strike agent, came to Stanley Junction. He demanded that the men on the Great Northern engage in a sympathetic strike until the other road was brought to terms. The older, wiser hands laughed at him. Jim Evans had returned to Stanley Junction, and at once joined in a movement to disrupt the local union by favoring the strike in question.

Evans had done a good deal of swaggering and threatening around the roundhouse that day, Ralph had just learned, and had intimidated some of the new hands into joining in the strike movement. He had left word that, as men came in from their runs, they were to report at a hall where the strikers met and announce which side of the contest they favored.

"Here we are, lad," said the veteran engineer, as they started up the stairs of a building on Railroad Street. "Don't look very business-like, those pails of beer going into that hall yonder and that cloud of tobacco smoke. I wouldn't stir a foot, only it's quite regular according to union rules to call and report in a matter like this."

"What are you going to do, Mr. Griscom?" asked Ralph.

"Short and sweet, give my sentiments and leave these loafers to fight it out among themselves."

"Include mine," said Ralph. "I do not understand these strike complications and I know you do, so I shall follow your guidance."

When they entered the hall they found a noisy crowd, smoking, playing cards and lounging about. On a platform sat Jim Evans, looking profoundly important. He sat at a table with a heap of papers before him. Griscom approached him, Ralph by his side.

"Who's in charge here?" demanded the old engineer gruffly.

"I am," announced Evans, in a somewhat unsteady tone. "Head of the movement."

"That so?" muttered Griscom. "Movement can't amount to much, then. Now then, Jim Evans, just one word. We came here out of courtesy to the union. We are members in good standing, and we represent the majority. At the meeting last night we voted you out as seceders. I am authorized to inform you that from now on no attention whatever will be paid to your crowd here."

"Is that so?" sneered Evans. "I reckon we'll attract some attention when we get in action. We have started our own union. We are going to break up the old one. Whoever comes in now to help us holds his job. Whoever don't, will get downed somewhere along the line, and don't you forget it."

"Being in the wrong," predicted Griscom steadily, "you won't succeed."

"Will you sign the roll?"

"No."

"Nor Fairbanks?"

"Let the lad speak for himself," said Griscom.

"I know little about these complications, Mr. Evans," said Ralph. "I pay my dues, and we are upheld in our positions by the central union. In the present instance I stand by the regular men."

Evans angrily picked up a sheet of paper. He scribbled upon it hastily.

"Know what that means?" he demanded.

"We don't, and are not at all anxious to know," retorted Griscom, turning to leave the hall.

"It means that you are blacklisted!" shouted Evans, rising to his feet. "As to you, Fairbanks, I owe you one, and the time has come when I am in power. Think twice—join us, or it will be the worse for you."

"Come on, lad," directed Griscom.

"Men," roared Evans to his mob of friends, "those two are on the black list. Notice them particularly, and hit hard when you strike."

Ralph went home somewhat disturbed by the episode, but not at all alarmed. He knew that such complications were frequent among the unions. His mother, however, was quite worried over the affair.

"That fellow Evans is a bad man, and has a personal hatred for you, Ralph," she said. "Besides that, as we know, he has been incited to make you trouble by Mr. Farrington. Be careful of yourself, my son, for I fear he may try to do you some mischief."

"I can only go on in the clear path of duty," said Ralph sturdily.

The next morning the roundhouse was in quite a tumult. Its vicinity was picketed by the strikers. Ralph entered the place to find Tim Forgan, the foreman, in a state of great excitement and worry. There were not men enough for the regular runs.

"Take out your regular train," he said to Griscom, "but I believe it will be annulled and new orders issued at the city end of the line. We're in for trouble, I can tell you. The strikers make some pretty bad threats, and you want to watch every foot of the route until this strike is settled one way or the other."

"There is no other way except to oppose these loafers boldly," pronounced Griscom. "The union has expelled them, and they are on the basis of rioters."

"Well, the railroad company will make some move to protect its property," said Forgan. "They must give us more men, though, or we will have to annul half the daily trains."

The Limited Mail got out of the yards with some difficulty. They had a spiked switch to look out for, and a missile from an old building smashed the headlight glass. At the limits a man tossed a folded paper into the locomotive cab. It was a poor scrawl containing direful threats to anyone opposing the new union.

When they reached the terminus Griscom found a committee of men from the central union waiting for him. They held a consultation. Then a messenger from the railway office came after him. It was a busy day for the veteran rail-roader.

"I don't like the looks of things," he said to Ralph, as they started on the homeward run. "The central union backs us, and the company is bound to fight the strikers to a finish. A lot of men are going down to take the places of the strikers. We are carrying them on this train, and serious trouble will begin as soon as the new men go to work."

Two days later the freight traffic of the Great Northern was practically tied up. The situation had become positively alarming. The strikers had gathered strength of numbers through intimidation, and the coming of new workers had aroused animosity.

Car loads of perishable fruits and the like were rotting in the yards, men were beaten, engines crippled, orders mixed up, crown sheets burned and cars smashed on open switches.

The Limited Mail was annulled as a regular train, and Griscom and Ralph and all other passenger employes placed on the irregular list. One day a man would take out the Mail, the next day he would be running freight empties to the city.

Some cars on siding along the route had been set on fire, and Griscom and Ralph were ordered down the line to pick up freight strays and haul them to the yards at Dover. It proved an unpleasant task. Strikers annoyed them in every way possible. Finally with a mixed train of about twenty cars they arrived at Afton, and took the sidings to gather in half-a-dozen gondolas.

The spot was remote from the main tracks. Ralph had to do the coupling. He had run back, bound on this duty in the present instance, when, just as he reached the end of their train, three ill-appearing men stepped into view from a dismantled switch shanty.

"Drop your signaling," spoke one of the three, advancing menacingly towards Ralph.

"Hardly," responded Ralph calmly, "seeing we want these cars."

"You don't take them," retorted the man, placing himself between the halted train and the cars beyond.

Ralph calmly gave the signal to the engine. The train backed. The man had to jump quickly out of the way. Ralph set the coupling pin, gave a quick signal and sprang into the first empty car. The man who had spoken to him followed him through the opposite open doorway.

"Fetch him out!" cried his two companions, running along the side of the car. "Maul him, and send him back to Stanley Junction as a lesson to the others."

The man attempted to seize Ralph and the latter resisted. The fellow called to his companions, and they sprang into the car. Ralph, trying to reach the doorway to leap out, was tripped up, and he fell quite heavily.

"Toss him out!" growled his first assailant, but Ralph recovered himself, managed to gain his feet, and leaped to the ground outside.

The three men followed. Ralph ran behind a pile of railroad ties. His pursuers gained upon him. He stumbled, fell flat, and they pounced upon him.

"Hold on there," suddenly spoke a new voice. "Get back and stay back, or I'll know the reason why."

Something whizzed through the air. It was a heavy cudgel. Whack! whack! whack! the three fellows retreated as their shoulders were assailed good and hard.

Ralph in some surprise regarded his new friend. He was a queer-looking old man, carrying a formidable cudgel, and this he now brandished recklessly in the faces of his adversaries, beating them back step by step.

"Now, you mind your own business," he warned the men. "Pitching onto a boy—three big loafers that you are!"

The men were cowards and sneaked sullenly away. Ralph's rescuer went back to the pile of ties and took up a little open memorandum book lying there.

Ralph noticed that its pages bore a list of numbers, as of cars.

"I am very grateful to you," said the young fireman.

"That's all right," responded the stranger, and ran his eye over the cars as they passed by as if looking at their numbers. Ralph concluded that he had some business on the spot.

"Are you in the service of the railroad?" he asked.

"Yes," nodded the man—"of many railroads. I am a professional car finder."

CHAPTER XV

THE RUNAWAY TRAINS

Ralph and his companion followed the train till it left the siding, when the young fireman set the switch and they stood by the side of the track until the locomotive backed down to where they were.

"Going into Dover?" inquired the man who had rendered Ralph such signal service.

"Yes," nodded Griscom, looking the questioner over suspiciously, as was his custom with all strangers recently since the strike began.

"Give me a lift, will you? I am through with my work here," observed the man. "My name is Drury. I am a car finder."

"Indeed?" said the old engineer with some interest of manner. "I've heard of you fellows. Often thought I'd like the job."

"You wouldn't, if you knew its troubles and difficulties," asserted Drury with a laugh, as he climbed into the tender. "You think it's just riding around and asking a few questions. Why, say, I have spent a whole month tracing down two strays alone."

"That so?" said Griscom.

"Yes, it is true. You see, cars get on a line shy of them, and they keep them purposely. Then, again, cars are lost in wrecks, burned up, or thrown on a siding and neglected. You would be surprised to know how many cars disappear and are never heard of again."

This was a new phase in railroad life to Ralph, and he was greatly interested. He plied the man with questions, and gained a good deal of information from him.

"Switch off here, Fairbanks," ordered Griscom, as they neared a siding.

"Is your name Fairbanks?" asked the carfinder of Ralph.

"It is."

"Heard of you," said Drury, glancing keenly at the young fireman. "It was down at Millville, last week. They seem to think a good deal of you, the railroad men there."

"I hope I deserve it," said Ralph modestly.

"Took a meal at a restaurant kept by a friend of yours," continued the carfinder.

"You mean Limpy Joe?"

"Exactly. Original little fellow—spry, handy and accommodating. Met another genius there—Dallas."

"Zeph? Yes," said Ralph. "He has got lots to learn, but he has the making of a man in him."

"He has. He was greatly interested in my position. Wanted me to hire him right away. Said he knew he could find any car that was ever lost. I gave him a job," and Drury smiled queerly.

"What kind of a job?" inquired Ralph.

"Oh, you ask him when you see him," said Drury mysteriously. "I promised to keep it a secret," and he smiled again. "Good-bye, I leave you here."

"Now then," said Griscom to his young assistant, "orders are to run to Ridgeton and start out in the morning picking up strays between there and Stanley Junction."

When they got to Ridgeton, it had begun to rain. It was a lonely station with a telegraph operator, and a few houses quite a distance away. The operator was not on duty nights since the strike. The engine was sidetracked. They got a meal at the nearest house, and the operator gave them the key to the depot, where he said they could sleep all night on the benches. This Griscom insisted on doing, in order that they might keep an eye on the locomotive.

They sat up until about nine o'clock. Then, tired out with a hard day's work, both soon sank into profound sleep. It was some time later when both, always vigilant and easily aroused, awoke together.

"Oh," said the old engineer drowsily, "only the ticker."

"Yes, some one is telegraphing," answered Ralph, "but it is a hurry call."

"Understand the code, do you?"

"Yes," answered Ralph. "Quiet, please, for a moment. Mr. Griscom, this is urgent," and Ralph arose and hurried to the next room, where the instrument was located.

He listened to the sharp ticking of the little machine. There was the double-hurry call. Then came some sharp, nervous clicks.

"R-u-n-a-w-a-y," he spelled out.

"What's that?" cried Griscom, springing to his feet.

"J-u-s-t p-a-s-s-e-d W-i-l-m-e-r, s-i-x f-r-e-i-g-h-t c-a-r-s. S-t-o-p t-h-e-m a-t R-i-d-g-e-t-o-n, o-r t-h-e-y w-i-l-l m-e-e-t N-o. f-o-r-t-y-e-i-g-h-t."

Ralph looked up excitedly. Griscom stood by his side. His eyes were wide awake enough now.

"Repeat that message—quick, lad!" he said in a suppressed tone. "Can you signal for repeat?"

Ralph did so, once more spelling out the message as it came over the wire.

"No. 48?" spoke Griscom rapidly. "That is the special passenger they have been sending out from Stanley Junction since the strike. What is the next station north? Act! Wire north to stop the train."

Ralph got the next station with some difficulty. A depressing reply came. No. 48 had passed that point.

"Then she's somewhere on the thirty-mile stretch between there and here," said Griscom. "Lad, it is quick action—wind blowing a hurricane, and those freights thundering down a one per cent. grade. Bring the lantern. Don't lose a moment. Hurry!"

Ralph took the lead, and they rushed for their locomotive. The young fireman got a red lantern and ran down the track, set the light, and was back to the engine quickly.

"This is bad, very bad," said Griscom. "Nothing but this siding, ending at a big ravine, the only track besides the main. The runaway must have a fearful momentum on that grade. What can we do?"

Ralph tested the valves. He found sufficient steam on to run the engine.

"I can suggest only one thing, Mr. Griscom," he said.

"Out with it, lad, there is not a moment to lose," hurriedly directed the old engineer.

"Get onto the main, back down north, set the switch here to turn the runaways onto the siding."

"But suppose No. 48 gets here first?"

"Then we must take the risk, start south till she reaches the danger signals, and sacrifice our engine, that is all," said Ralph plainly.

It was a moment of intense importance and strain. In any event, unless the unexpected happened, No. 48 or their own locomotive would be destroyed. On the coming passenger were men, women and children.

"Duty, lad," said Griscom, in a kind of desperate gasp. "We must not hesitate. Pile in the black diamonds and hope for the best. If we can reach the creek before the runaways, we can switch them onto a spur. It means a smash into the freights there. But anything to save the precious lives aboard the night passenger from Stanley Junction."

They ran on slowly, then, gaining speed, got a full head of steam on the cylinders. At a curve the bridge lights came into view.

"What do you see?" demanded Griscom, his band trembling on the throttle, wide open now.

"She's coming," cried Ralph. "I caught the glint of the bridge lights. She's not six hundred yards away."

It was a desperate situation now. Both engineer and fireman realized this. The backward swing was caught, and down the course they had just come their locomotive sped with frightful velocity.

It was a mad race, but they had the advantage. One mile, two miles, three miles, the depot, down the main, and before the engine had stopped, Ralph was on the ground. He ran to the switch, set it, and then both listened, watched and waited.

"There are the runaways," said Ralph.

Yes, there they were, speeding like phantoms over the rain-glistening steel. Nearer and nearer they came, passed the siding, struck the switch, ran its length, and then a crash—and the night passenger from Stanley Junction was saved!

"I don't know what the damage will be," muttered Griscom in a long-drawn breath of relief, "but we have done our duty as we saw it."

They got back on the siding and removed the red lights before No. 48 arrived. The night passenger sped tranquilly by, her train crew little dreaming of the peril they had escaped.

The next afternoon, when they arrived at Stanley Junction, the assistant superintendent of the road highly commended their action in regard to the runaway freights.

Ralph went home tired out from strain of work and excitement. As he neared the house he noticed a wagon in the yard and a horse browsing beside it.

"Why," he said, "that rig belongs to Limpy Joe."

Ralph hurried into the house. He found both Joe and Zeph in the sitting room. They were conversing with his mother, with whom the cripple boy had always been a great favorite.

"Well, fellows, I am glad to see you," said Ralph heartily, "but what brought you here?"

"Plainly," replied Limpy Joe—"Ike Slump."

"Why, what do you mean?" inquired the young fireman.

"I mean that we have been burned out," said Joe, "and Ike Slump did it."

CHAPTER XVI

CAR NO. 9176

"Burned out!" exclaimed Ralph, deeply concerned.

"Yes," nodded Joe, a trifle dolefully. "Labors of years in ashes—Limpy Joe's Railroad Restaurant a thing of the past."

"How did it happen?"

"Spite work. Three nights ago, late in the evening, Ike Slump appeared at the restaurant and demanded a free meal. I gave it to him. Then he demanded some money, and I refused it. He became bold and ugly, and told us how his crowd had it in for us, that they knew I had some hand in helping you get that stolen plunder, and would fix us sooner or later. He advised me to buy them off. I sent him away. Last night we discovered the place on fire, and it was burned to the ground."

Ralph was deeply distressed over his friend's misfortune. The lame fellow, however, was undaunted. He deplored his loss, but he was by no means discouraged.

"Thankful to have the horse and wagon left," he said. "I can always earn a living with that. Besides that, we saw Van Sherwin the other day. He is getting on finely, and I think we could get work on the Short Line Railroad. For the present, though, I am going to stay at Stanley Junction. I have a dozen plans for getting a little money together. Will you try us as boarders for a week or two, Ralph?"

"I answered that question a few minutes ago," reminded Mrs. Fairbanks, "and if you two will sleep in the same room, you will cause no inconvenience whatever."

"And you, Zeph?" said Ralph, turning to the farmer boy.

Zeph had been strangely silent. He appeared to be trying to look very dignified and much absorbed in thought.

"Oh, me?" he said now. "Why, I'm already at work. Commence to-night. Call boy at the roundhouse. Old one is with the strikers. Mr. Forgan engaged me this afternoon."

"Why, that is fine," said Ralph. "A start in the right direction. Look out for the strikers, though, Zeph."

"Don't fret about me," advised Zeph. "I'm a fighter when aroused. See, here is my list to call in the morning," and he showed Ralph a slip of paper containing about a dozen names.

Ralph read it over, and after a meal went out with Zeph and showed him the location of the homes of those named in the list.

"This job is all right," said Zeph, as they returned to the house, "but it is only a sort of side line with me."

"Indeed?" smiled Ralph, amused at the off-hand, yet self-important manner of his companion.

"Oh, yes."

"How is that?"

"Simply want to get into the service so as to have the privilege of riding around on engines when I want to. It sort of introduces me, you see."

"What do you want to ride around on engines for?" asked Ralph. "You can't afford to waste your time that way."

"Waste my time? waste my time?" repeated Zeph. "Huh, guess you don't know what you're talking about! I'm on the trail of a big fortune."

"You don't say so."

"I do. Ralph Fairbanks, I'll let you into the secret. You've been a good friend to me, and you shall help me."

"What ridiculous nonsense are you talking, Zeph?"

"You'll see whether it's nonsense or not when some day I walk in on you with a fortune. Now, this is on the dead quiet, Fairbanks?"

"Oh, sure," laughed Ralph.

"Very well. I met a fellow the other day, who is a car finder."

"Mr. Drury, you mean?" asked Ralph.

"How did you know?" questioned Zeph in surprise.

"He told me he had met you, and agreed with me that you were a pretty fair kind of a fellow."

"Did he?" said Zeph, very much pleased at the double compliment. "Well, I got interested in his business and he finally gave me a—a—well a job, you might call it."

"Salary big, Zeph?"

"No salary at all," responded Zeph. "It's a partnership deal. If I find certain property, I am to have a big reward to divide with him."

"What kind of property?"

"Diamonds."

"Oh, going digging for them?"

"Don't make fun of me, Fairbanks," said Zeph in a slightly offended tone. "This is a fair and square business proposition. About five years ago a car was lost, presumably on the Great Northern. At least, it can be traced no farther than the terminus of the Midland Central, where it was switched onto this line here. There all trace of it was lost."

"Valuable freight aboard?"

"No, on the contrary, it was empty, but, all the same, between sealed boards and the rough ones a pocketbook containing a lot of valuable diamonds was hidden."

"Who by?"

"A traveling jewelry salesman named Isaacs."

"What did he hide it there for?"

"He had to. You see, he was on another railroad line and crossing some tracks when some footpads assaulted him. He managed to escape and got into the empty car I told you about. Then he heard them coming to search for him, and hid the diamonds in a break of the boards at one side of the car."

"I see."

"They dragged him out, beat him into insensibility and stole all his money. He woke up in a hospital a month later, after a siege of fever. The first thing he thought of was the diamonds and the car. He had taken particular pains to note the number of the car."

"What was it, may I ask?"

"Confidentially?"

"Of course."

"It belonged to the Southern Air Line Road, and its number was 9176."

"Why, you are telling a very interesting story," declared Ralph, now really interested in the same. "He searched for the car, of course?"

"At once. He telegraphed everywhere; he advertised; he employed detectives. It was no use. During the month of his illness, car No. 9176 had disappeared."

"That looks mysterious."

"The car finder says not at all. Such things happen frequently. But it went somewhere, didn't it? It may be lying on some old siding, in some creek after a wreck, stolen by gravel pit men, or in service still on some line. One thing is sure, if in existence still, it must be on one of four railroad lines, and the Great Northern is one of those roads."

"What do you propose to do?" inquired Ralph.

"Go over every one of those lines carefully."

"But Mr. Drury has done that already, has he not?"

"What of it? A first search doesn't always bring results. He has given me full details as to the car, and, according to the records, it was lost on the Great Northern. In a day or two I am going to have a look at the transfer records at Dover. Then I am going to look up the trainmen who probably hauled the car. Oh, I have a theory and a plan. If I find the car I shall be almost rich."

"Not a bad prospect, Zeph," said Ralph, "but if I were you I would stick at regular work and make the search for that car a secondary matter."

"You'll remember it and help me out if you can?" asked Zeph.

"Surely I will," and Ralph made a note of the number of the car in his memorandum book.

When the young fireman arose the next morning, he found Zeph seated on the front porch lounging back in an easy chair and his face all bandaged up. Mrs. Fairbanks stood near by, regarding her guest solicitously.

"Why, what is the matter, Zeph?" inquired Ralph in profound surprise.

"Whipped four men, that's all," answered Zeph with a smile that was almost ghastly, for his lips were all cut and swollen up, one eye disfigured and two teeth gone. "I went on my rounds this morning. I made sure to wake up the fellows on call, and one of them threatened to kill me if I ever came to his door again with that 'fog-horn holler' of mine, as he called it. The night watch-man said he'd arrest me for disturbing the peace. I didn't mind that. Then I ran across four strikers. They wanted me to join them. I refused, and—that's all, except that I'll bet they are worse off than I am, if it was four to one."

"Going to keep right on at your job?" inquired Ralph.

"Am I?" cried the undaunted Zeph. "Well, if anything would make me it would be this attack on me. Tell you, Fairbanks, hot times are coming. Forgan was on duty all night, and he told me this morning to advise you to be extra cautious in coming to work. The strikers are in an ugly mood, and they are going to make a bold break to smash up things to-day, they threaten."

"Yes," sighed Ralph, "affairs must come to a crisis sooner or later, I fear. Duty is plain, though. I shall stick to Griscom, and Griscom insists that he will stick to the road."

Mrs. Fairbanks looked anxious and frightened. Turning to enter the house, the young fireman started violently and his mother and Zeph uttered exclamations of excitement.

A terrific explosion had rent the air. Its echoes rang out far and wide, and its source seemed to be the railroad depot.

"Oh, Ralph! what does that mean?" cried Mrs. Fairbanks.

"I fear," said Ralph seriously, "the strikers are rioting and the trouble has begun."

CHAPTER XVII

UNDER SEALED ORDERS

The young fireman was soon headed for the railroad yards. A good many people were bound hurriedly in the same direction, for the explosion had aroused the town.

As he neared the place, he could hear considerable shouting. He came to the tracks at a point where there was a switch shanty. The man on duty looked worried and scared.

"What is the trouble?" inquired Ralph.

"The strikers have blown up a freight car with dynamite," replied the flagman. "They have threatened me, old and feeble as I am. I'm afraid I'll have to lay off till this trouble is over."

In the distance Ralph saw the mere skeleton of a freight car. It was in flames, and a number of men were pushing other cars from its vicinity to prevent them from catching on fire. A man tapped him on the shoulder. Turning, Ralph recognized one of the strikers.

"See here, Fairbanks," he said, "I'm of the decent sort, as you know, but I think our position is right."

"Does that look like it?" demanded the young fireman, pointing to the burning car.

"I'm not responsible for that," said the man, "and I can't prevent the hot-headed ones from violence. I know you won't join us, but I'm just friendly enough to give you a warning. Don't go on duty to-day."

"I certainly shall, if I am needed," replied Ralph. "Your union is in bad hands, and can't last."

The man shrugged his shoulders and Ralph passed on his way. A piece of coal came whizzing through the air a few minutes later from the vicinity of a crowd of loiterers. It knocked off the young fireman's cap. He picked it up and walked slowly on.

When he came to the roundhouse, he found the doors shut. Most of the windows in the place were broken in. Several target rods near by lay on the ground, and at a glance Ralph saw that considerable damage had been wrought during the night.

"There must be a crisis soon," he said, and went to the roundhouse door. Before he was admitted several stones rained about him, thrown from behind a pile of ties. Inside, Ralph found Griscom and several others among the older engineers and firemen. All hands looked serious, the foreman particularly so.

"Glad you came," said Forgan. "There's bad trouble brewing. The strike has reached the danger point. We can't run any regulars from the depot and won't try to to-day, but the Limited Mail must go to terminus. Griscom is ready for the run; are you? The regular engineer and fireman say they won't risk their lives."

"I did not see the train anywhere," observed Ralph.

"There is to be no regular train, only one postal and one express car. They will back down here in half-an-hour from the limits. Here is a wire for you. Came early this morning."

With some surprise Ralph read a brief telegram. It came from the headquarters of the Great Northern in the city, was signed by the president of the road, and read:

"Come to my office immediately on reaching terminus."

Ralph showed this to Griscom. The situation was discussed by the men in the roundhouse, and the time passed by until a sharp whistle announced the arrival of the Limited Mail.

As Griscom and Ralph went outside to relieve those temporarily in charge of the locomotive, they were pelted from several points with pieces of dirt, iron and coal. A crowd surged up to the engine. Then a startling thing occurred that dispersed them more quickly than they had gathered.

As if by magic there appeared on the platforms of the two coaches fully a dozen guards armed with rifles. The train now proceeded on its way without molestation. At the limits the guards left it to protect other railroad property.

The only trouble experienced during the run was between Afton and Dover, when some missiles were thrown and two switches found spiked. When they reached the city, Ralph tidied up and went to see the president of the road.

Mr. Grant received him with a pleasant smile, beckoned him to a comfortable seat, and, closing the door of his private office, said:

"Fairbanks, we think a good deal of you, and I know you deserve that favorable opinion. There are many trusted and reliable men in our service, but they do not think as quickly as you do. You are familiar with people at Stanley Junction, and on that account I wish you to do an important service for us."

"I shall be pleased to," said Ralph.

"It is this: Some one is working against us, some one is undermining us. We now believe that the sympathetic strike, as it is called, is more the result of some plot than a genuine sentiment of unionism. A man named Delmay, from the Midland Central, and a man named Evans, a discharged employe

73

of our road, are at the head of the movement. Both are persons of bad record in every way."

"I know that," murmured Ralph.

"We believe that these men are hired to promote the strike."

"Why, by whom, Mr. Grant?" inquired Ralph in considerable surprise.

"That we wish you to find out. All we suspect is that some outside party is inciting them to the strike to carry out some selfish personal ends. You must find out who he is. You must discover his motives."

Ralph was perplexed. He could not understand the situation at all.

"I will do all I can in the line you suggest, sir," he said, "although I hardly know where to begin."

"You will find a way to make your investigation," declared the president of the Great Northern. "I rely a great deal upon your ability already displayed in ferreting out mysteries, and on your good, solid, common sense in going to work cautiously and intelligently on a proposition. You can tell Forgan you are relieved on special service and wire me personally when you make any discoveries."

Ralph arose to leave the room.

"Wait a moment," continued Mr. Grant, taking up an envelope. "I wish you to hand this to Griscom. The Limited Mail will not make any return trip to-night. Instead, a special will be ready for you. You need mention this to no one. That envelope contains sealed orders and is not to be opened until you start on your trip. The superintendent of the road will see you leave and will give you all further instructions needed."

There was a certain air of mystery to this situation that perplexed Ralph. He reported to Griscom, who took the letter with a curious smile.

"Must be something extra going on down the road," he observed. "Wonder what? Start after dark, too. Hello, I say—the pay car."

They had come to the depot to observe an engine, two cars attached, and the superintendent standing on the platform conversing with a man attired in the garb of a fireman.

The latter was a sturdy man of middle age, one of the best firemen on the road, as Ralph knew. He nodded to Griscom and Ralph, while the superintendent said:

"Fairbanks, this man will relieve you on the run."

Ralph looked surprised.

"Why," he said, "then I am not to go on this trip?"

"Oh, yes," answered the official with a grim smile,—"that is, if you are willing, but it must be as a passenger."

Ralph glanced at the passenger coach. Inside were half-a-dozen guards.

"Not in there," replied the superintendent, "We want you to occupy the pay car here. Everything is ready for you."

"All right," said Ralph.

"Come on, then."

The superintendent unlocked the heavy rear door of the pay car, led the way to the tightly sealed front compartment, and there Ralph found a table, chair, cot, a pail of drinking water and some eatables.

"You can make yourself comfortable," said the official. "There will probably be no trouble, but if there is, operate this wire."

The speaker pointed to a wire running parallel with the bell rope to both ends of the train. On the table lay a rifle. The only openings in the car were small grated windows at either end.

The official left the car, locking in Ralph. The young fireman observed a small safe at one end of the car.

"Probably contains a good many thousands of dollars," he reflected. "Well, here is a newspaper, and I shall try to pass the time comfortably."

By getting on a chair and peering through the front ventilator, Ralph could obtain a fair view of the locomotive. The train started up, and made good time the first thirty miles. Then Ralph knew from a halt and considerable switching that they were off the main rails.

"Why," he said, peering through the grating, "they have switched onto the old cut-off between Dover and Afton."

That had really occurred, as the young fireman learned later. The officials of the road, it appeared, feared most an attack between those two points, and the sealed orders had directed Griscom to take the old, unused route, making a long circuit to the main line again.

Ralph remembered going over this route once—rusted rails, sinking roadbed, watery wastes at places flooding the tracks. He kept at the grating most of the time now, wondering if Griscom could pilot them through in safety.

Finally there was a whistle as if in response to a signal, then a sudden stop and then a terrible jar. Ralph ran to the rear grating.

"Why," he cried, "the guard car has been detached, there are Mr. Griscom and the engineer in the ditch, and the locomotive and pay car running away."

He could look along the tracks and observe all this. Engineer and fireman had apparently been knocked from the cab. Some one was on the rear platform of the pay car, a man who was now clambering to its roof. The guards ran out of the detached coach and fired after the stolen train, but were too late.

Rapidly the train sped along. Ralph ran to the front grating. The locomotive was in strange hands and the tender crowded with strange men.

"It's a plain case," said Ralph. "These men have succeeded in stealing the pay car, and that little safe in the corner is what they are after."

The train ran on through a desolate waste, then across a trestle built over a swampy stretch of land. At its center there was a jog, a rattle, the tracks gave way, and almost with a crash, the train came to a halt.

It took some time to get righted again, and the train proceeded very slowly. Ralph had done a good deal of thinking. He knew that soon the robbers would reach some spot where they would attack the pay car.

"I must defeat their purpose," he said to himself. "I can't let myself out, but—the safe! A good idea."

Ralph settled upon a plan of action. He was busily engaged during the next half hour. When the train came to a final stop, there was an active scene about it.

Half-a-dozen men, securing tools from the locomotive, started to break in the door of the pay car. In this they soon succeeded.

They went inside. The safe was the object of all their plotting and planning, but the safe was gone, and Ralph Fairbanks was nowhere in the pay car.

CHAPTER XVIII

THE STRIKE LEADER

Ralph felt that he had done a decidedly timely and clever act in outwitting the train robbers. He had left the car almost as it stopped, and under the cover of the dark night had gained the shelter of the timber lining the track.

The young fireman waited until the men came rushing out of the car. They were dismayed and furious, and, leaving them in a noisy and excited consultation, Ralph started back towards the trestle work.

"They won't get the safe, that is sure," said the young railroader in tones of great satisfaction, as he hurried along in the pelting storm. "They will scarcely pursue me. It is pretty certain, however, that they will be pursued, and I may meet an engine before I reach Dover."

Just as he neared the end of the trestle Ralph saw at some distance the glint of a headlight. It was unsteady, indicating the uncertain character of the roadbed.

"About two miles away," decided the young fireman. "I must manage to stop them."

With considerable difficulty, Ralph secured sufficient dry wood and leaves in among some bushes to start a fire between the rails and soon had a brisk blaze going. The headlight came nearer and nearer. A locomotive halted. Ralph ran up to the cab.

It contained Griscom, the city fireman and two men armed with rifles. The old engineer peered keenly at the figure, quickly springing to the step of the engine.

"You, lad?" he cried heartily. "I'm glad of that. Where is the train?"

"About two miles further on beyond the trestle."

"And the pay car?"

"The robbers were in possession when I left them."

"Then they will get away with the safe!" cried the engineer excitedly.

"Hardly," observed Ralph, with a smile.

"Eh, lad, what do you mean?"

"What I say. Truth is, I saw what was coming. There was only one thing to do. There were tools in the car. I sawed a hole through the floor of the car, rolled the safe to it, and dumped it through. It went between two rotten ties, and lies in the swamp—safe."

With a shout of delight old John Griscom slapped his young assistant admiringly on the shoulder.

"Fairbanks," he cried, "you're a jewel! Mate," to the fireman, "this is glad news."

"It is, indeed," said his companion. "I wouldn't like the record of losing that safe. Can you locate the spot, Fairbanks?"

"It may take some trouble," answered Ralph. "The best thing to do is to get a wrecking car here; meantime, the trestle should be guarded."

They ran on and up to the spot where the stolen train was halted, but found the vicinity deserted. It seemed that whatever the robbers had guessed out as to the mystery of the safe, they did not consider there was any chance of recovering it.

The two men armed with rifles remained at the trestle, while the others took the stolen pay car back to Dover. Once there, Griscom kept the wires busy for a time. About daylight a wrecking crew was made up. Ralph accompanied them to the scene of the attempted robbery.

He could fairly estimate the locality of the sunken safe, and some abrasions of the ties finally indicated the exact spot where the safe had gone through into the water below. It was grappled for, found, and before noon that day the pay car train arrived at Stanley Junction with the safe aboard.

Affairs at the terminal town were still in an unsettled condition. The presence of armed guards prevented wholesale attacks on the railroad property, but there were many assaults on workmen at lonely spots, switches tampered with and shanty windows broken in.

Ralph reported to Tim Forgan and then went home. He went to sleep at once, awoke refreshed about the middle of the afternoon, and then told his mother all the occurrences of that day and the preceding one.

While Mrs. Fairbanks was pleased at the confidence reposed in her son by the railroad authorities, she was considerably worried at the constant turmoil and dangers of the present railroad situation. Ralph, however, assured her that he would take care of himself, and left the house trying to form some plan to follow out the instructions of the president of the Great Northern.

He could not go among the strikers, and without doing so, or sending a spy among them, it would be difficult to ascertain their motives and projects. Coming around a street corner, the young fireman halted abruptly.

A procession of strikers was coming down the street. They were a noisy, turbulent mob, cheered on by like rowdyish sympathizers lining the pavements.

"Why, impossible!" exclaimed Ralph, as he noticed by the side of Jim Evans, the leader of the crowd, his young friend, Zeph Dallas.

The latter seemed to share the excitement of the paraders. He acted as if he gloried in being a striker, and the familiar way Evans treated him indicated that the latter regarded him as a genuine, first-class recruit.

Zeph caught Ralph's eye and then looked quickly away. The young fireman was dreadfully disappointed in the farmer boy. He went at once to the roundhouse, where the foreman told him that Zeph had deserted the afternoon previous.

"I don't understand it," said Forgan. "The lad seemed to hate the strikers for attacking him the other night. I suppose, though, it's with him like a good many others—there's lots of 'relief money' being given out, and that's the bait that catches them."

"I must manage to see Zeph," mused Ralph. "I declare, I can hardly believe he is really on their side. I wonder how near I dare venture to the headquarters of that mob."

The young fireman went to the vicinity of the hall occupied by the strikers, but he did not meet Zeph. Then Ralph proceeded to the business portion of Stanley Junction. He visited the bank and several other leading local business institutions. He made a great many inquiries and he felt that he was on the edge of some important discoveries.

When he got home he found Zeph sitting on the porch, smiling as ever. Ralph nodded seriously to him. Zeph grinned outright.

"What's that kind of a welcome for, eh?" he demanded.

"Sorry to see you in the ranks of the strikers to-day, Zeph," observed Ralph.

"Ought to be glad."

"What?"

"I suppose a fellow is free to follow out his convictions, isn't he?"

"Certainly."

"Well, I'm following out mine," declared Zeph—"the conviction that of all the mean rascals in this burg, Jim Evans is the meanest. See here, Fairbanks, have you lost your wits? Do you really for one minute suppose I sympathize with those fellows?"

"You seemed pretty close to Evans."

"Grand!" chuckled Zeph. "That's just what I was working for. See here, I made up my mind that those fellows were up to more mischief than what they have already done. I concluded there was something under the surface of this pretended strike. I wanted to find out. I have."

Ralph looked very much interested now. He began to see the light.

"Go on, Zeph," he said.

"Well, I found out just what I suspected—some one is furnishing the strikers with money, and lots of it."

"Do you know who it is?"

"I don't, but I do know one thing: every day Evans goes to the office of a certain lawyer in town here. They have a long consultation. Evans always comes away very much satisfied and with more money."

"What's the lawyer's name, Zeph?" inquired Ralph.

"Bartlett."

Just then they were called in to supper by Mrs. Fairbanks. Ralph was silent and thoughtful during most of the meal.

The young fireman had learned that afternoon that a stranger named Bartlett had been buying up all the stock of the railroad he could secure. The man was not in good repute at Stanley Junction. He had come there only the week previous, Ralph was told, and occupied a mean little room in the main office building of the town.

After supper Ralph strolled down town. He entered the building in question and ascended its stairs. He knew the occupants of most of the offices, and finally located a room which contained a light but had no sign on the door.

Footsteps ascending the stairs caused the young fireman to draw back into the shadow. A man came into view and knocked noisily at the closed door.

"Here I am, Bartlett," said the fellow, lurching about in an unsteady way.

"I see you are," responded the man inside the room, "primed for work, too, it seems to me."

Ralph could not repress some excitement. The man Bartlett he instantly recognized as the person who had delivered to him in the city the papers from Gasper Farrington. His visitor he knew to be a discharged telegraph operator of the Great Northern.

"Yes," said the latter, as the door closed on him, "I'm ready for work, so bring on your wire-tapping scheme soon as you like."

CHAPTER XIX

THE WIRE TAPPERS

When the door of the office that Ralph was watching closed again and was locked, the young fireman approached the room. He was very sure that some important move against the railroad was meditated by the two men he had just seen, and he was anxious to overhear their conversation if possible.

To his intense satisfaction Ralph found that a coal box rested under the clouded-glass window of the office looking into the hallway. This window was down from the top some inches. Ralph clambered up on the coal box, got to the side of the window, fixed his eye at a small space where the glass was broken, and prepared to listen to the words of the two men he had in view.

Both sat in chairs now. Bartlett looked brisk and pleased; the ex-telegraph operator was unkempt, rather sullen, and acted like a man under orders on some unpleasant duty.

"Well, Morris," said the former, "all ready, are you? Tools and wire in that bag?"

"Batteries and all, complete outfit," responded the other. "What's the programme?"

"You haven't mentioned about my employing you to any one?"

"Certainly not."

"And have arranged to stay away from town for several days?"

"A week, if you like, at ten dollars a day you promised me," answered Morris.

"Very good. Let me see. There's a train about 10 o'clock."

"There is, if the strikers will let it run out," said Morris.

"Oh, they will. I have arranged all that," chuckled Bartlett. "They'll even help it on, knowing I'm aboard."

"That so?" muttered Morris. "You must have a pull somewhere."

"I have, or at least money has, and I control the money," grinned Bartlett. "You are to come with me down the line about twenty miles. You'll be told then about this special job."

Bartlett got up and bustled about. He packed a great many papers in a satchel, and finally announced that they had better be starting for the depot.

"Any little by-play you see on the train," said Bartlett, "help along, mind you."

"Why, what do you mean?" inquired Morris.

"You'll see when we get there," replied Bartlett enigmatically.

When they reached the depot the two men got aboard the one passenger coach of the night accommodation. There was a combination express car ahead. Ralph went to the messenger in charge and arranged to have free access to do as he desired.

When the train started up, he opened the rear door of the car and commanded a clear view into the passenger coach. The men he was watching sat side by side, engaged in conversation. There were only a few passengers aboard.

Ralph kept his eye on the two men. He noticed that Bartlett consulted his watch frequently and glanced as often from the car window. Finally, when the brakeman was out on the rear platform and the conductor at the front of the coach, the young fireman saw Bartlett quickly draw a small screwdriver from his pocket. Hiding its handle in his palm and letting the blade run along one finger, he dropped his arm down the seat rail into the middle of the aisle.

Morris watched towards the rear platform, Bartlett kept his eye on the conductor. His hand worked against the floor of the car. Finally he drew up his arm, put the screwdriver in his pocket and once more resumed his watch on the outside landscape.

There was a sharp signal, and the train gave a jerk. Bartlett arose to his feet. The next instant he fell flat headlong, and lay apparently insensible on the floor of the coach.

The conductor ran outside. The train started up again. Ralph, from the open doorway, heard the engineer shout back something about a false signal, presumably the work of the strikers. The train proceeded on its way.

It was not until then, as he re-entered the coach, that the conductor became aware of the prostrate man on the floor and Morris and other passengers gathering around him in excitement and solicitude. Ralph ventured across the platform near to the door of the passenger coach.

Bartlett, seemingly unconscious, was lifted to a seat. He soon opened his eyes, but feigned intense pain in his side, and acted the injured man to perfection. He began to explain, pointing to the floor. The conductor investigated. Ralph saw him draw a long brass screw into sight.

"A clever game," murmured the young fireman. "What a rascal the fellow is! He is laying the foundation for a damage suit."

Morris made himself busy, taking the names of witnesses. When the train stopped, Bartlett had to be almost lifted from the coach. Ralph alighted, too, and kept in the shadow. As soon as the train left, Bartlett was able to walk about unassisted.

The little town they had arrived at was dark and silent, and the two men met no one as they proceeded down its principal street. Then they turned to the south and walked a distance of about a mile. There was a kind of a grove lining the railroad. At its center they reached a lonely hut.

"Open up, there!" shouted Bartlett, pounding on its door with a stick he had picked up.

A light soon showed through the cracks of the board shutters.

"Who is there?" demanded a voice from the inside.

"Bartlett."

"All right—come in."

"Gasper Farrington," murmured Ralph, as he recognized the occupant of the hut.

It was the magnate of Stanley Junction, still disguised, just as he had been the last night Ralph had seen him at the home of Jim Evans. The three men disappeared within the house. Ralph approached and went cautiously about the place. He could not find a single point where he could look into the hut.

The young fireman felt that it was very important that he should learn what was going on within the house. He at length discovered a way of gaining access to at least one part of it. This was at the rear where a high stack of old hay stood. It almost touched the hut, and its top was very near to a sashless aperture in the attic.

Ralph scaled the stack with some difficulty and reached its top. In another moment he was inside the attic. It was low, the rafters were few and far between, and, as he crept over these, they began to sway and creak in an alarming way.

"This won't do at all," murmured the youth in some dismay, for it seemed that one more movement would carry down the entire ceiling below. He tried to retreat. There was a great cracking sound, and before he could help himself the young fireman went sprawling into the room below in the midst of a shower of plaster and laths.

"Hello!" shouted Bartlett, jumping up from a chair in consternation.

"I should say so," exclaimed Morris, dodging about out of the way of falling bits of plaster from the ceiling.

"A spy!" cried Farrington, "a spy! Why, it's Ralph Fairbanks!"

The young fireman stood surrounded by the three men, trying to clear his half-blinded eyes. He was seized and hustled about, thrown into a chair, and regained his wonted composure to find Gasper Farrington confronting him with an angry face.

"So, it's you, is it—you, again?" spoke the latter, gazing at Ralph with a glance full of ill will.

"Yes," responded the youth. "I can't deny it very well, can I?"

"How do you come to be up in that attic? How long have you been there? What are you up to, anyway?" shouted the excited Farrington.

"Don't ask me any questions for I shall not answer them," retorted Ralph nervily. "Here I am. Make the best of it."

"See here," said Bartlett, a deep frown on his face. "This looks bad for us. Morris, watch that young fellow a minute or two."

He and Farrington went into the next room. There was a low-toned consultation. When they came back the lawyer carried a piece of rope in his hand. It was useless for Ralph to resist, and the three men soon had him securely bound. He was carried into a small adjoining room, thrown on a rude mattress, and locked in.

For nearly half-an-hour he could hear the drone of low voices in the adjoining room. Then the door was unlocked, and Farrington came in with a light and made sure that the captive was securely bound.

"You are going to leave here, then?" asked Bartlett.

"Don't I have to?" demanded Farrington. "This fellow has located us. I'll take you and Morris to the place I told you about, and move my traps out of here early in the morning."

"What are you going to do with Fairbanks?" inquired Bartlett.

"I'm thinking about that," retorted Farrington in a grim way. "It's the chance of a lifetime to settle with him. You leave that to me."

The speakers, shortly after this, left the hut with Morris. Ralph found he could not release himself, and patiently awaited developments. His captors had left the light in the next room and the door open, and he could see on a table the satchel the lawyer had brought with him from his office.

The sight of it caused Ralph to make renewed efforts for freedom. He strained at his bonds strenuously. Finally a strand gave way.

It was just as he began to take hope that he might acquire his liberty before his captors returned, that a sudden disaster occurred that made the young fireman fear for his life.

Some more of the ceiling plastering fell. It struck the lamp on the table, upset it, and in an instant the room was ablaze.

CHAPTER XX

IN PERIL

The young fireman gave a great shout of distress and excitement as he realized that he was in a decidedly perilous predicament. The oil of the lamp had ignited and the hut seemed doomed.

Ralph tugged at his bonds in a frenzy. Another strand of the rope gave way, then another, and still another. He trembled with mingled surprise and hope. Could he get free in time? It seemed not, for the flames were spreading fast and furiously.

Suddenly there was a shout outside of the hut. It was repeated, and then there came a great crash at the door. Ralph wondered at this, for he could think only of Farrington and his accomplices returning to the rescue. The loud pounding on the door, however, indicated that the persons engaged in it had no key. There was more than one person; Ralph ascertained this from the sound of mingled voices.

Suddenly the door gave way. It was burst bodily from its hinges and went crashing against the blazing table, upsetting it. At just that moment Ralph got one arm free. He was about to shout for assistance when he recognized the intruders.

They were Ike Slump and Mort Bemis. Both dashed into the blazing room. One found a pail of water and threw it in among the flames. This subdued the blaze partially.

"Be quick!" cried Slump to his companion. "Grab all you can. You have been watching the place, and say you know where old Farrington is likely to hide his valuables."

"Right here," replied Bemis, tearing open the door of a cupboard. "Here's a satchel."

"And here's another one," said Ike Slump, picking up the one that Bartlett had brought to the place. "Look sharp, now. They may come back at any moment."

The two marauders ransacked the room. Ralph refrained from calling out to them. He could now reach his pocket knife, and just as Slump and Bemis, pretty well singed by the flames, ran out of the hut, he hurried to a rear door and darted outside as well.

The young fireman peered around the corner of the hut. He saw Slump and Bemis making for the nearest timber. Ralph put after them, and as he gained the cover of the woods, looking back, he made out three figures dashing towards the blazing hut.

"Farrington and the others," decided Ralph. "This is an exciting business. Now to keep track of Slump and Bemis. I can hardly figure out, though, how they came to rob the hut, for Farrington was once their friend."

The precious pair of thieves scurried along through the woods, laughing and talking gleefully over the plunder they had secured. They must have gone over three miles before they halted. It was at a spot in among high bushes. Here they had evidently been camping previously, for there was a lot of hay on the ground, the signs of a recent campfire, and a sort of roof of bark overhead for shelter from rain and dew. They sat down on the ground and Slump proceeded to light a lantern.

"Your watching has amounted to something at last, Mort," said Slump. "Farrington went back on us in a measly way. Why, after all we did for him he took up with Jim Evans and others, and even refused me a few dollars when we were in hiding and trouble after that silk robbery. Here's our revenge. He's been up to some deep game for a week. He'll never know who stole this plunder."

"Find how much of it there is," suggested Bemis.

Each took up a satchel to investigate the contents. Ralph was intensely interested. He peered from a safe covert near at hand.

"Well, well, well!" exclaimed Slump as he opened the satchel taken from the cupboard of the old hut. "Why, there's a fortune here, if we can only handle it. Bonds of the Great Northern, stock in the Great Northern. See? some money—notes, mortgages, deeds! This is a big find."

"Same here, except the money," reported Bemis, investigating the documents in the satchel brought from Stanley Junction by Bartlett. "Mostly railroad stock in the Great Northern. Private letters, lists of names of the strikers. Memoranda about some wire-tapping scheme. Say, these papers are enough to send the old skeesicks to the penitentiary. He'll pay a fortune to get them back."

Slump pocketed the ready cash in the satchel. Then he was silently thoughtful for a few moments.

"See here, I have my scheme," he said finally. "We'll carry these satchels down to the old barge at the creek, and hide them there. Then we'll block out some plan to work Farrington for their return."

"All right," said Bemis. "Come ahead."

They took up the satchels and started on again, and Ralph followed them as before. They came to a creek, and, after lining its shore for nearly a mile, to a large roughly-made scow. Both boarded the craft, disappeared in its hold, reappeared, and came to the shore again.

"We'll just enjoy the ready cash for the time being," said Slump, "and later find out a safe way to deal with Farrington."

When they had gone, Ralph went aboard the scow. A scuttle led down into its hold. Its cover was closed with a strong spring bolt. Ralph drew this back and sat over the edge of the scuttle.

He peered down, prepared to push the cover clear back, when he slipped and went below head-long. The cover fell tightly shut, and he was a prisoner.

Ralph did not mind this much at the time. He believed he could readily force up the cover in some way when he wanted to leave the scow. He lit some matches and proceeded to search for the two satchels. He found them in a remote corner of the hold.

It was when he prepared to leave the hold that the young fireman discovered himself in a decided quandary. He could barely reach the scuttle cover, and there was not an object in the hold that he could use to force it open. Finally Ralph decided that he could not hope for escape in that direction.

There was a little window at one end of the scow, but it was too small to escape by. Ralph was compelled to accept the situation, at least until daylight. He tried to sleep, and at dawn looked out from the window.

"I will simply have to wait here until some one passes by," he told himself. "In the meantime, though, Slump and Bemis may return. Can I reach the rope holding the scow to the shore?"

This was secured around a tree stump. Ralph reached with his pocket knife through the window, and began cutting at the scow end of the rope, which ran just above it.

In a few minutes the strands gave way and the scow floated down the creek.

CHAPTER XXI

A FRIEND IN NEED

There was a sluggish current to the creek and as soon as the scow got into midstream, it proceeded steadily on its voyage.

"This is better than staying at the old mooring place," reasoned Ralph. "Of course, Slump and Bemis will return there and search for the scow. Before they do, I hope I will have drifted past some house or settlement where I can call out for assistance."

Ralph, however, was not destined to meet with ready relief. The scow floated along banks wild and timbered, and, during a vigilant watch at the little window of over two hours, he saw no human being or habitation.

Finally the scow slowed up, its course became irregular, it bumped into some obstacle, turned around, and Ralph discovered the cause of the stoppage. A mass of logs and other debris had formed clear across the creek at one point. This the scow lined, edging slowly along as if drawn by some counter-current.

In a few minutes the craft had worked its way into a cut-off from the creek. It floated slowly in among a swampy wilderness of reeds and stunted trees, came to halt at a shallow, and there remained stationary.

"Why, this is worse than being in the creek," ruminated Ralph, with some concern. "There was a chance of hailing some one there sooner or later, but in this isolated spot I stand the risk of starving to death."

The young fireman was both hungry and thirsty. He made another desperate attempt to force the scuttle, but found it an utter impossibility. Then he took out his pocket knife. There was one last chance of escape in sight. If he could cut the wood away around the bolt of the scuttle cover, he might force it open.

Ralph could not work to any advantage, for the top of the hold was fully a foot above his head. However, patiently and hopefully he began his task. Bit by bit, the splinters and shavings of wood dropped about him.

"Too bad, that ends it," he exclaimed suddenly, as there was a sharp snap and the knife blade broke in two.

The situation was now a very serious one. Ralph tried to view things calmly, but he was considerably worried. He was somewhat encouraged, however, a little later, as he noticed that along the dry land lining the swampy cut-off there were signs of a rough wagon road.

"All I can do now is to watch and wait," he declared. "I guess I will take a look over the contents of those satchels."

Once started at the task, Ralph became greatly interested. He was amazed at what the documents before him revealed of the plans and villainies of old Gasper Farrington. There was evidence enough, indeed, as Slump had said, to send the village magnate to the penitentiary.

"This information will be of great value to the railroad people," said Ralph. "It would enable them to at once break the strike."

"Whoa!"

Ralph gave utterance to a cry of delight and surprise. He ran to the little window of the scow. Not fifty feet away was a horse and wagon. Its driver had shouted out the word to halt. Now he dismounted and was arranging a part of the harness where it had come loose.

"Hello, there! Joe! Joe! hurry this way!" fairly shouted Ralph.

"Hi, who's that, where are you?" demanded the person hailed.

"In the scow. Ralph! Locked in! Get me out!"

"I declare! It can't be Ralph. Well! well!"

Nimbly as his crutches would allow him, Limpy Joe came towards the scow. He halted as he neared the window where he could make out the anxious face of his friend.

"What are you ever doing there? How did you get in there? Why, this is wonderful, my finding you in this way," cried the cripple.

"I'll tell you all that when I get out," promised Ralph. "All you have to do is to spring back the bolt catch on the cover to the hold scuttle."

"I'll soon have you out then," said Joe, and with alacrity he waded into the water, got aboard the old craft, and in another minute Ralph had lifted himself free of his prison place.

"Whew! what a relief," aspirated the young fireman joyfully. "Joe, it is easy explaining how I came to be here—the natural sequence of events—but for you to be on hand to save me is marvelous."

"I don't see why," said Joe. "I have been coming here for the last three days."

"What for?" inquired Ralph.

"Business, strictly."

"Mother told me you had taken the horse and wagon and had gone off on a peddling trip," said Ralph.

"Yes, I sold out a lot of cheap shoes to farmers which I got at a bargain at an auction," explained Joe. "Then I struck a fine new scheme. It brought me here. I'll explain to you later. Your story is the one that interests me. Tell me how you came to be in that scow, Ralph."

The young fireman brought up the two satchels from the hold of the old craft, and briefly related to Joe the incidents of his experience with Farrington, Slump and the others.

"I say, you have done a big thing in getting those satchels," said Joe, "and you want to place them in safe hands at once. Come ashore, and I'll drive you to the nearest railroad town. You don't want to risk meeting any of your enemies until you have those papers out of their reach."

When they came up to the wagon, Ralph gazed at its piled-up contents in surprise. The wagon bottom was filled with walnuts and butternuts. There must have been over twelve bushels of them. On top of them was spread a lot of damp rushes and all kinds of wild flowers, mosses and grasses. Two large mud turtles lay under the wagon seat.

"Why, what does all that layout mean?" exclaimed Ralph, in amazement.

"That," said little Joe, with sparkling eyes, "is an advertising scheme. Some time ago I discovered the finest nut grove in the timber yonder you ever saw. I suppose I could in time have gathered up a hundred wagon loads of them. I intend to make a heap of money out of them. A couple of days ago, though, I thought out a great idea. You know Woods, the dry goods man at the Junction?"

"Yes," nodded Ralph.

"He is a wide-awake, enterprising fellow, and I told him of my scheme. It caught his fancy at once. The plan was this: every week, I am to trim up his show window with what we call 'a nature feature.' We keep pace with vegetation. This week we show a swamp outfit; next week pumpkins and the like; the following week autumn leaves. We work in live objects like turtles to give motion to the scene. Do you catch on?"

"It is an excellent idea and will attract lots of attention," declared Ralph.

"You bet it will," assented his comrade with enthusiasm. "Anyhow, my pay is fine and I expect to work other towns in the same way. I will show you the most artistic display window you ever saw when I get this load of truck to town."

In about two hours they reached a railroad station, and somewhat later Ralph caught a train for the city. He went at once to the office of the president of the Great Northern. There was a long interview. As Ralph left the railroad magnate his face was pleased and his heart light and hopeful.

"Fairbanks," said Mr. Grant, "I cannot express my satisfaction at your discoveries. It is as we supposed—some individual has been encouraging the strikers. There are ample proofs among these papers of the fact that Gasper Farrington has hired the strikers to commit all kinds of misdeeds to scare stockholders of the road. He has thus been enabled to buy up their stock at a reduced figure, to make an enormous profit when the strike is over. He had a scheme to tap our wires and cause further complications and trouble. Within a week the backbone of the strike will be broken, and we shall not forget your agency in assisting us to win out."

Ralph went back to Stanley Junction that same day. He related all his varied adventures to his mother that evening.

"One thing I discovered from those documents in the satchels," said Ralph. "Farrington has transferred all his property to Bartlett so we could not collect the money he owes us."

"Then we shall lose our twenty thousand dollars after all," said Mrs. Fairbanks anxiously.

"Wait and see," replied Ralph, with a mysterious smile. "I am not yet through with Gasper Farrington."

CHAPTER XXII

THE LIMITED MAIL

"All aboard!"

The conductor of the Limited Mail gave the signal cheerily. Ralph swung in from his side of the cab on the crack locomotive of the road. Old John Griscom gave a chuckle of delight and the trip to the city began.

It was ten days after the adventure in the scow—ten days full of activity and progress in the railroad interests of the Great Northern. This was the morning when old-time schedules were resumed and every part of the machinery of the line went back to routine.

"I tell you, lad, it feels good to start out with clear tracks and the regular system again. I'm proud of you, Fairbanks. You did up those strikers in fine style, and it will be a long time before we shall have any more trouble in that line."

"I hope so, Mr. Griscom," said Ralph. "The company seems determined to teach the strikers a lesson."

This was true. Immediately after the visit of Ralph to the city, the railroad people had set at work to make the most of the evidence in their hands. A statement of the facts they had discovered was given to the public, a series of indictments found against Gasper Farrington, Bartlett, Jim Evans and others, and a vigorous prosecution for conspiracy was begun. Among the most important witnesses against them was Zeph Dallas. Farrington and Bartlett disappeared. Evans and the others were sent to jail.

A great revulsion in popular sentiment occurred when the true details of the strike movement were made known. The respectable element of the old union had scored a great victory, and work was resumed with many undesirable employes on the blacklist.

It seemed to Ralph now as though all unfavorable obstacles in the way of his success had been removed. He believed that Slump and Bemis were powerless to trouble him farther. As to Farrington, Ralph expected at some time to see that wily old schemer again, for the railroad was in possession of papers of value to the discredited railroad magnate.

Ralph had now become quite an expert at his work as a fireman. There was no grumbling at any time from the veteran engineer, for Ralph had a system in his work which showed always in even, favorable results. The locomotive was in splendid order and a finer train never left Stanley Junction. At many stations cheers greeted this practical announcement of the end of the strike.

There was no jar nor break on the route until they reached a station near Afton. The engine was going very fast, when, turning a curve, Griscom uttered a shout and turned the throttle swiftly.

"Too late!" he gasped hoarsely.

The young fireman had seen what Griscom saw. It was an alarming sight. At a street crossing a baby carriage was slowly moving down an incline. A careless nurse was at some distance conversing with a companion. The shrill shriek of the whistle caused her to discover the impending disaster, but she had become too terrified to move.

Ralph readily saw that speed would not be greatly diminished by the time the locomotive overtook the child in the baby carriage, and in a flash he acted. He was out on the running board and onto the cowcatcher so quickly that he seemed fairly to fly. Grasping a bracket, the young fireman poised for a move that meant life or death for the imperiled child.

The locomotive pounded the rails and shivered under the pressure of the powerful air brakes. Ralph swung far down, one hand extended. The baby carriage had rolled directly between the rails and stood there motionless.

It contained a beautiful child, who, with an innocent smile, greeted the approaching monster of destruction as if it were some great, pleasing toy. Ralph's heart was in his throat.

"Grab out!" yelled Griscom, fairly beside himself with fear and suspense.

The young fireman's eyes were dilated, his whole frame trembled. Quick as lightning his hand shot out. It met in a bunch of the clothing of the child. He lifted; the vehicle lifted, too, for a strap held in its occupant.

There was a terrific tension on the arm of the young railroader. The lower part of the vehicle was crunched under the cowcatcher and the child was almost borne away with it. Then the pressure lightened. With a great breath of relief and joy Ralph drew the child towards him, tangled up in the wreckage of the baby carriage.

The train stopped. Griscom did not say a word as they backed down. His face was white, his eyes startled, his breath came hard, but he gave his intrepid young assistant a look of approbation and devotion that thrilled Ralph to the heart.

A crowd had gathered around the distracted nurse at the street crossing. She was hysterical as the rescued child was placed in safety in her arms. Other women were crying. A big policeman arrived on the scene. Griscom gave the particulars of the occurrence.

"Name, please?" said the officer to Ralph.

"Oh, that isn't necessary at all," said Ralph.

"Isn't it? Do you know whose child that is?"

"No," said Ralph.

"The father is Judge Graham, the richest man in the town. Why, he'd hunt the world over to find you. A lucky fellow you are."

Ralph gave his name and the train proceeded on its way amid the cheers of the passengers, who had learned of the brave act of the young fireman. When terminus was reached, a fine-looking old lady approached the locomotive.

"Mr. Fairbanks," she said to Ralph, "the passengers desire you to accept a slight testimonial of their appreciation of your bravery in saving that young child."

Ralph flushed modestly.

"This looks like being paid for doing a simple duty," he said, as the lady extended an envelope.

"Not at all, Mr. Fairbanks. It was a noble act, and we all love you for it."

"I think more of that sentiment than this money," declared Ralph.

The envelope contained fifty dollars. Griscom told the story of the rescue all over Stanley Junction next day, and the local newspapers made quite an article of it.

The next morning Ralph had just completed his breakfast, when his mother went to the front door to answer the bell. She showed some one into the parlor and told Ralph that a gentleman wished to see him.

The young fireman was somewhat astonished, upon entering the parlor, to be grasped by the hand and almost embraced by a stranger.

"I am Judge Graham," spoke the latter, in a trembling, excited tone. "Young man, you saved the life of my only child."

"I was glad to," said Ralph modestly.

The judge went on with a description of the joy and gratitude of the mother of the child, of his sentiments towards Ralph, and concluded with the words:

"And now, Mr. Fairbanks, I wish to reward you."

"That has been done already," said Ralph, "in your gracious words to me."

"Not at all, not at all," declared the judge. "Come, don't be modest. I am a rich man."

"And I a rich mother in having so noble a son," spoke Mrs. Fairbanks, with deep emotion. "You must not think of a reward, sir. He will not take it."

After a while the judge left the house, but he did so with an insistent and significant declaration that "he would not forget" Ralph.

The young fireman was surprised to see him returning a few minutes later, in the company of two of his own friends, Mr. Trevor, the nephew of the president of the Great Northern, and Van Sherwin.

"Well, this is a queer meeting," cried Van with enthusiasm, as they entered the house. "Here we met Judge Graham, who is a great friend of Mr. Trevor, and the very man we wished to see."

This statement was soon explained. It appeared that Mr. Trevor had fully recovered his health, and had come to Stanley Junction with Van to make preparations to issue and sell the bonds of the Short Cut Railroad. The judge was one of the friends he had intended to interview about buying some bonds.

For an hour young Trevor recited to Judge Graham the prospects of the little railway line and their plans regarding the same. Ralph was fascinated at his glowing descriptions of its great future.

Ralph's visitors went away, but in a short time Van returned to the cottage.

"I say, Ralph," he remarked, "Judge Graham is going to invest in those bonds."

"That's good," said Ralph.

"And I heard him tell Mr. Trevor to put down an extra block of them in the name of Ralph Fairbanks."

CHAPTER XXIII

THE PICNIC TRAIN

Zeph Dallas had returned to work. His connection with the strikers had been fully explained to the railroad people by Ralph, and the farmer boy was readily taken back into the service of the company. Zeph boarded with Mrs. Fairbanks, and Limpy Joe did, too, when he was in Stanley Junction.

The enterprising Joe was winning his way famously. His advertising scheme was a grand success, and the nuts he gathered brought in a good many dollars. One day he came to town to announce that he was going to move his traps, thanking Mrs. Fairbanks for her great kindness to him in the past.

"Are you going to leave the Junction permanently, Joe?" asked Ralph.

"I think so," answered the cripple. "You see, I have been up to the headquarters of the Short Line Railroad. They can use my horse and wagon. They offer me a good salary to cook for them, and the concession of running a restaurant when their line is completed."

"A good opportunity, that, Joe," said Ralph, "although the main prospect you mention is far in the future, isn't it?"

"Not at all," declared Joe. "I guess you haven't kept track of proceedings in The Barrens. Their telegraph line is clear through, both ways from headquarters now. The bonds are nearly all sold, and they expect to begin to lay the rails in earnest next week."

"I noticed a good deal of activity at our end of the line," said Ralph. "I think the scheme is going to be a success. I almost wish I was going to work with you fellows."

It was now drawing on towards late fall. For several weeks the young fireman had not been disturbed by his enemies. Work had gone on smoothly. He was learning more and more every day, and his savings amounted to quite a pretentious sum.

The only outside issue that troubled Ralph was the fact that they had not yet recovered the twenty thousand dollars due his mother from old Gasper Farrington. That individual had disappeared. Ralph kept a sharp lookout, for upon finding the magnate and bringing him to terms depended the last chance of getting the money.

There was the last picnic of the season one day, and Ralph had been assigned to duty to look after things generally. He was surprised when Forgan took him off the run of the Limited Mail.

"It will be a sort of vacation holiday for you, lad," said the roundhouse foreman. "We want somebody reliable to look after the train, with so many women and children aboard. You will be boss over the engineer, fireman and the whole train crew for the day."

"Quite an important commission," said Ralph, "but what will the train crew say about it?"

"Oh, they will be glad to work with the responsibility on somebody else. Here is the schedule. Be careful of your running time, Fairbanks. I wouldn't have anything happen to the picnic train for worlds."

Ralph studied out the situation. When the train left Stanley Junction he took a position in the locomotive, attended to reports at all stations they passed, and the train reached the picnic grounds in safety and was run on the siding.

Ralph gave himself up to the enjoyment of a real holiday. He knew nearly everybody on the picnic grounds and nearly everybody there knew him. About the middle of the afternoon a boy living at the Junction came up to him.

"Say, Ralph," he remarked, tendering the young fireman a note. "A fellow out in the woods gave me this for you."

Ralph took the missive, and, opening it, read its contents with mingled surprise and suspicion. The note ran:

"If R. F. wants to hear of something to his advantage, come to the old railroad bridge right away."

There was no signature to the scrawl, but Ralph quite naturally thought of Ike Slump and his crowd. That did not, however, deter him from going to keep the appointment. He cut a stout cudgel and proceeded to the old railroad bridge named in the note.

The young fireman glanced keenly about him, but for some time did not get a view of anybody in the vicinity. Finally from a clump of bushes up the incline a handkerchief waved. Ralph climbed the embankment to find himself facing Ike Slump.

The latter was ragged and starved-looking. To Ralph it appeared that the ex-roundhouse boy had been having a decidedly hard time of it recently.

"You needn't carry any stick around here," said Slump, sullenly. "You needn't be afraid of me."

"Not at all," answered Ralph, "although your actions in the past would warrant my having a whole battery around me."

"That's done with," asserted Slump, quite meekly. "Bemis is up there a little ways. You needn't be afraid of him, either."

"What are you getting at with all this talk, Ike?" inquired Ralph.

"Why, we want to be friends."

"What for?"

"Because—because we're tired of starving and being hunted and the like," said Slump. "You have won out, we are beaten. We want to work together."

"I declare I don't understand what you are driving at," said Ralph. "Come, Ike Slump, play no more crafty games. It don't pay. Be honest and straight. What did you bring me here for?"

"To make some money for both of us."

"In what way?"

"You would give a good deal to find Gasper Farrington, wouldn't you, now?"

"I certainly am anxious to locate that man, yes," answered Ralph frankly.

"All right, we know where he is."

"And you are willing to make amends, I suppose, for your past misconduct by telling me where Farrington is to be found, so that I can have him arrested."

"Well, I guess not!" cried Mort Bemis, coming upon the scene. "We want pay for what we do. We want a hundred dollars to begin with. A lot more when you get that money he owes you."

"My friends," said Ralph, promptly turning from the spot. "Not a cent. I don't believe you know how to act square. You don't show it by your present proposition. If you really want to be helped, and if you are sorry for your past wrong doing, come back to Stanley Junction, tell the truth, take your punishment like men, and I will be your good friend."

"Well, you're a bold one," sneered Slump, getting very angry. "You won't help us out, then?"

"With money—on your promise? No. I shall find Gasper Farrington finally without your aid, and, if you have nothing further to say, I shall return to the picnic grounds."

"I don't think you will," said Bemis, roughly placing himself in Ralph's path.

"Why not?" inquired the young fireman calmly, grasping his cudgel with a closer grip.

"Because—say, Ike, grab him, quick! If he won't deal with us and we can get him a prisoner, Farrington will pay us. You know he always wanted to get rid of him."

Ralph prepared to meet the enemy squarely. Slump and Bemis rushed towards him. Before they could begin the fight, however, a man burst through the underbrush whom Ralph recognized as a Stanley Junction police officer detailed on picnic duty.

"Found you, my friends, have I?" he hailed the two fellows. "Grab one of them, Fairbanks, I've got the other. I was on the lookout for them. They stole a purse from the basket of an old lady in the picnic grounds a few hours ago. Slump? Bemis? Well, you are a fine pair, you are!"

The officer insisted on arresting them, the more so that upon recognizing them now he suddenly remembered that a reward had been offered for their apprehension by the railroad company. The crestfallen plotters were taken to the train and locked up in one end of the express car.

Ralph went to them after a spell and tried to learn something more from them, but they were now sullen and vengeful.

In due time the train was backed down to the main track, the engine detached made a run for water, and, returning, stood some little distance from the cars.

The fireman and engineer left the engine to help their families gather up their traps and take them aboard the train. Ralph was busy in the cab. He was looking over the gauges when a sudden blow from behind stretched him insensible on the coal of the tender.

As he slowly opened his eyes Ralph saw Slump and Bemis in the cab. In some way they had escaped, had stolen the locomotive, and were speeding away to liberty.

"Just heard a whistle. It must be the Dover Accommodation," Slump was remarking. "Get off and open the siding switch, Mort."

This Bemis did, and the engine started up again. Ralph thrilled at the words Slump had spoken. He was weak and dizzy-headed, but he made a desperate effort, staggered to his feet and sprang from the cab.

Had the locomotive remained at the picnic grounds, the train would have been switched to the siding again until the Accommodation passed. As it was, unwarned, the Accommodation would crash into the train.

Ralph heard its whistle dangerously near. He looked up and down the tracks. Ahead, a bridge crossed the tracks, and near it was a framework with leather pendants to warn freight brakemen in the night time. Towards this Ralph ran swiftly. Weak as he was, he managed to scale the framework, gained its center, and sat there panting, poised for the most desperate action of his young career.

The Accommodation train came into view. Ralph sat transfixed, knowing that he would soon face death, but unmindful of the fact in the hope that his action would save the lives of those aboard the picnic train.

The Accommodation neared him. The young fireman got ready to drop. He let go, crashed past the roof of the cab, and landed between the astonished engineer and fireman.

"The picnic train—on the main, stop your locomotive!" he panted, and fainted dead away.

CHAPTER XXIV

IN "THE BARRENS"

Ralph Fairbanks had taken a terrible risk, and had met with his first serious accident since he had commenced his career as a young fireman. When he next opened his eyes he was lying in his own bed, a doctor and his mother bending solicitously over him.

Slowly reason returned to him. He stared wonderingly about him and tried to arise. A terrible pain in his feet caused him to subside. Then Ralph realized that he had suffered some serious injury from his reckless drop into the locomotive cab near the picnic grounds.

"What is it, doctor?" he asked faintly.

"A bad hurt in one arm and some ugly bruises. It is a wonder you were not crippled for life, or killed outright."

"The train—the picnic train!" cried Ralph, clearly remembering now the incidents of the stolen engine.

"The Accommodation stopped in time to avert a disaster," said Mrs. Fairbanks.

Ralph closed his eyes with a satisfied expression on his face. He soon sank into slumber. It was late in the day when he awoke. Gradually his strength came back to him, and he was able to sit up in bed.

The next day he improved still more, and within a week he was able to walk down to the roundhouse. Forgan and all his old friends greeted him royally.

"I suppose you have the nerve to think you are going to report for duty," observed Forgan. "Well, you needn't try. Orders are to sick list you for a month's vacation."

"I will be able to work in a week," declared Ralph.

"Vacation on full pay," continued the roundhouse foreman.

Ralph had to accept the situation. He told his mother the news, and they had a long talk over affairs in general. The doctor advised rest and a change of scene. The next day Van Sherwin called on his way back to The Barrens. That resulted in the young fireman joining him, and his mother urged him to remain with his friends and enjoy his vacation.

A recruit to the ranks of the workers of the Short Cut Railroad presented himself as Ralph and Van left for the depot one morning to ride as far as Wilmer. This was Zeph Dallas.

"No use talking," said the farmer boy. "I'm lonesome at Stanley Junction and I'm going to join Joe."

"All right," assented Van, "if you think it wise to leave a steady job here."

"Why, you'll soon be able to give me a better one, won't you?" insisted Zeph. "It just suits me, your layout down there in The Barrens. Take me along with you."

When they reached Wilmer and left the train, Van pointed proudly to a train of freight cars on the Great Northern tracks loaded with rails and ties.

"That's our plunder," he said cheerily. "Mr. Trevor is hustling, I tell you. Why, Ralph, we expect to have this end of the route completed within thirty days."

As they traversed the proposed railroad line, Ralph was more and more interested in the project. Little squads of men were busily employed here and there grading a roadbed, and the telegraph line was strung over the entire territory.

They reached the headquarters about noon. A new sign appeared on the house, which was the center of the new railroad system. It was "Gibson."

A week passed by filled with great pleasure for the young railroader. Evenings, Mr. Gibson and his young friends discussed the progress and prospects of the railroad. There were to be two terminal stations and a restaurant at the Springfield end of the route. There were only two settlements in The Barrens, and depots were to be erected there.

"We shall have quite some passenger service," declared Mr. Gibson, "for we shorten the travel route for all transfer passengers as well as freight. The Great Northern people do not at all discourage the scheme, and the Midland Central has agreed to give us some freight contracts. Oh, we shall soon build up into a first-class, thriving, little railroad enterprise."

One evening a storm prevented Ralph from returning to headquarters, so he camped in with some workmen engaged in grading an especially difficult part of the route. The evening was passed very pleasantly, but just before nine o'clock, when all had thought of retiring, a great outcry came from the tent of the cook.

"I've got him, I've caught the young thief," shouted the cook, dragging into view a small boy who was sobbing and trembling with grief.

"What's the row?" inquired one of the workmen.

"Why, I've missed eatables for a week or more at odd times, and I just caught this young robber stealing a ham."

"I didn't steal it," sobbed the detected youngster. "I just took it. You'd take it, too, if you was in our fix. We're nearly starved."

"Who is nearly starved?" asked Ralph, approaching the culprit.

"Me and dad. We were just driven to pick up food anywhere. You've got lots of it. You needn't miss it. Please let me go, mister."

"No, the jail for you," threatened the cook direfully.

"Oh, don't take me away from my father," pleaded the affrighted youngster. "He couldn't get along without me."

"See here, cook, let me take this little fellow in hand," suggested Ralph.

"All right," assented the cook, adding in an undertone, "give him a good scare."

Ralph took the boy to one side. His name was Ned. His father, he said, was Amos Greenleaf, an old railroader, crippled in an accident some years before. He had become very poor, and they had settled in an old house in The Barrens a few miles distant. Ralph made up a basket of food with the cook's permission.

"Now then, Ned," said Ralph, "you lead the way to your home."

"You won't have me arrested?"

"Not if you have been telling me the truth."

"I haven't," declared the young lad. "It's worse than I tell it. Dad is sick and has no medicine. We have nearly starved."

It was an arduous tramp to the wretched hovel they at last reached. Ralph was shocked as he entered it. It was almost bare of furniture, and the poor old man who lay on a miserable cot was thin, pale and racked with pain.

"I am Ralph Fairbanks, a fireman on the Great Northern," said the young railroader, "and I came with your boy to see what we can do for you."

"A railroader?" said Greenleaf. "I am glad to see you. I was once in that line myself. Crippled in a wreck. Got poor, poorer, bad to worse, and here I am."

"Too bad," said Ralph sympathizingly. "Why have you not asked some of your old comrades to help you?"

"They are kind-hearted men, and did help me for a time, till I became ashamed to impose on their generosity."

"How were you injured, Mr. Greenleaf?" asked Ralph.

"In a wreck. It was at the river just below Big Rock. I was a brakeman. The train struck a broken switch and three cars went into the creek. I went with them and was crippled for life. One of them was a car of another road and not so high as the others, or I would have been crushed to death."

"A car of another road?" repeated Ralph with a slight start.

"Yes."

"You don't know what road it belonged to?"

"No. They recovered the other two cars. I never heard what became of the foreign car. I guess it was all smashed up."

"Gondola?"

"No, box car."

Ralph was more and more interested.

"When did this occur, Mr. Greenleaf?" he asked.

"Five years ago."

"Is it possible," said Ralph to himself, "that I have at last found a clew to the missing car Zeph Dallas and that car finder are so anxious to locate?"

CHAPTER XXV

TOO LATE

Two days later Ralph went down the line of the little railroad to where it met the tracks of the Great Northern. Mr. Gibson had sent him with some instructions to the men at work there, and at the request of the young fireman had assigned him to work at that point.

This consisted in checking up the construction supplies delivered by rail. Ralph had a motive in coming to this terminus of the Short Line Route. The information he had gained from the old, crippled railroader, Amos Greenleaf, had set him to thinking. He found Zeph Dallas working industriously, but said nothing about his plans until the next day.

At the noon hour he secured temporary leave of absence from work for Zeph and himself, and went to find his friend.

Zeph was a good deal surprised when Ralph told him that they were to have the afternoon for a ramble, but readily joined his comrade.

"Saw some friends of yours hanging around here yesterday," said the farmer boy.

"That so?" inquired Ralph.

"Yes, Slump and Bemis. Guess they were after work or food, and they sloped the minute they set eyes on me. Say, where are you bound for anyway, Ralph?"

"For Wilmer."

"What for?"

"I want to look around the river near there. The truth is, Zeph, I fancy I have discovered a clew to that missing freight car."

"What!" cried Zeph excitedly. "You don't mean car No. 9176?"

"I mean just that," assented Ralph. "Here, let us find a comfortable place to sit down, and I'll tell you the whole story."

Ralph selected a spot by a fence lining the railroad right of way. Then he narrated the details of his interview with Amos Greenleaf.

"Say," exclaimed Zeph, "I believe there's something to this. Every point seems to tally somehow to what information the car finder gave me, don't you think so? Besides, in investigating the matter, I heard about this same wreck. And five years ago? Ralph, this is worth looking up, don't you think so?"

Zeph was fairly incoherent amid his excitement. He could not sit still, and arose to his feet and began walking around restlessly.

"You see, it is a long time since the car disappeared," said Ralph, "and we may not be able to find any trace of it. The car finder, in his investigations, must have heard of this wreck. Still, as you say, it is worth following up the clew, and that is why I got a leave from work for the afternoon."

"Hello," said Zeph, looking in among the bushes abruptly, "some one in there? No, I don't see anybody now, but there was a rustling there a minute or two ago."

"Some bird or animal, probably," said Ralph. "Come on, Zeph, we will go to the bridge and start on our investigations."

The river near Wilmer was a broad stream. It was quite deep and had a swift current. The boys started down one bank, conversing and watching out. Ralph laughed humorously after a while.

"I fancy this is a kind of a blind hunt, Zeph," he said. "We certainly cannot expect to find that car lying around loose."

"Well, hardly, but we might find out where it went to if we go far enough," declared Zeph. "I tell you, I shall never give it up now if I have to go clear to the end of this river."

They kept on until quite late in the afternoon, but made no discoveries. They passed a little settlement and went some distance beyond it. Then Ralph decided to return to the railroad camp.

"All right," said Zeph, "only I quit work to-morrow."

"What for?"

"To find that car. I say, I'm thirsty. Let us get a drink of water at that old farm house yonder."

They went to the place in question and were drinking from the well bucket when the apparent owner of the place approached them.

"Won't you have a cup or a glass, my lads?" he inquired kindly.

"Oh, no, this is all right," said Ralph.

"On a tramp, are you?" continued the farmer, evidently glad to have someone to talk to.

"In a way, yes," answered Ralph, and then, a sudden idea struck him, he added: "By the way, you are an old resident here, I suppose?"

"Forty years or more."

"Do you happen to remember anything of a wreck at the bridge at Wilmer about five years ago?"

"Let me see," mused the man. "That was the time of the big freshet. Yes, I do remember it faintly. It's the freshet I remember most though. Enough timber floated by here to build a barn. See that old shed yonder?" and he pointed to a low structure. "Well, I built that out of timber I fished ashore. Lumber yard beyond Wilmer floated into the creek, and all of us along here got some of it."

"What do you know about the wreck?" asked Ralph.

"Heard about it at the time, that's all. Sort of connect the freshet with it. That was a great washout," continued the farmer. "Even sheds and chicken coops floated by. And say, a box car, too."

"Oh," cried Zeph, with a start as if he was shot.

"Indeed?" said Ralph, with a suppressed quiver of excitement in his tone.

"Yes. It went whirling by, big and heavy as it was."

"Say, Mister, you don't know where that car went to, do you?" inquired Zeph anxiously.

"Yes, I do. I know right where it is now."

"You do?"

"Yes, old Jabez Kane, ten miles down the creek, got it. He is using it now for a tool shed."

"Oh!" again cried Zeph, trembling with suspense and hope.

Ralph nudged him to be quiet. He asked a few more questions of the farmer and they left the place.

"Ralph," cried Zeph wildly, "we've found it!"

"Maybe not," answered the young fireman. "It may not be the same car."

"But you're going to find out?"

"It's pretty late. We had better make a day of it to-morrow."

"All right, if we can't attend to it to-day," said Zeph disappointedly; and then both returned to camp.

Next morning early both started for the creek again. By proceeding across the country diagonally, they saved some distance.

It was about noon when they approached a rickety, old farmhouse which a man had told them belonged to Jabez Kane.

"There it is, there it is," cried Zeph, as they neared it.

"Yes, there is an old box car in the yard near the creek, sure enough," said Ralph.

They entered the farm yard. The box of the car they looked at sat flat on the ground. It had been whitewashed several times, it appeared, so they could trace no markings on it. They approached it and stood looking it over when a man came out of the house near by.

"Hey," he hailed, advancing upon them. "What you trespassing for?"

"Are we?" inquired Ralph, with a pleasant smile. "We mean no harm."

"Dunno about that," said the farmer suspiciously. "Was you here last night?"

"Oh, no," answered Ralph.

"Well, what do you want?"

"I was sort of interested in this old car," announced Ralph.

"Why so?" demanded Kane.

"Well, we are looking for a car that floated down the creek here about five years ago."

"For the railroad?" asked the farmer.

"In a way, yes, in a way, no."

"Does the railroad want to take it away from me?"

"Certainly not. They would like to know, though, if it's a car of the Southern Air Line and numbered 9176."

"You've got it, lad. This was just that car. What's the amazing interest in it all of a sudden? Look here," and he took them around to the other side of the car. "Last night two boys came here; my son saw them hanging around here. Then they disappeared. This morning I found the car that way."

Ralph and Zeph stared in astonishment. A four-foot space of the boards on the outside of the car had been torn away. At one point there was a jagged break in the inside sheathing. In a flash the same idea occurred to both of them.

"Too late!" groaned poor Zeph. "Some one has been here and the diamonds are gone."

Ralph was stupefied. He remembered the rustling in the bushes when they were discussing their plans the day previous. He believed that their conversation had been overheard by some one.

Ralph asked the man to send for his son, which he did, and Ralph interrogated him closely. The result was a sure conviction that Ike Slump and Mort Bemis had secured the diamonds hidden in the box car about five years previous.

CHAPTER XXVI

THE MAD ENGINEER

"Well, good-bye, Zeph."

"Good-bye, Ralph. Another of my wild dreams of wealth gone."

"Don't fret about it, Zeph."

"How can I help it?"

Ralph had decided to return home. He was now fully recuperated, and his vacation period would expire in a few days.

It was the evening of the day when they had discovered the missing box car only to find that others had discovered it before them. Ralph had arranged to flag a freight at the terminus of the Short Line Route and was down at the tracks awaiting its coming.

The freight arrived, Ralph clambered to the cab, waved his hand in adieu to Zeph, and was warmly welcomed by his friends on the engine.

They had proceeded only a short distance when a boy came running down an embankment. So rapid and reckless was his progress that Ralph feared he would land under the locomotive. The lad, however, grasped the step of the cab, and was dragged dangerously near to the wheels. Ralph seized him just in time and pulled him up into the cab.

"Well!" commented the engineer, "it's a good thing we were going slow. Here, land out as you landed in, kid."

"Please don't," cried the boy, gazing back with tear-filled eyes and trembling all over. "Please let me ride with you."

"Against the rules."

"See, there they are!" almost shrieked the boy, pointing to two men who came rushing down the embankment. "Oh, don't let them get me."

"Give him a show till I learn his story," said Ralph to the engineer, so the latter put on steam and the two men were outdistanced.

"Oh, thank you, thank you!" panted the boy, clinging close to Ralph.

"Come up on the water tank," said Ralph, "and I'll have a talk with you."

The lad, whom the young fireman had befriended, was a forlorn-looking being. He wore no shoes, was hatless, and had on a coat many sizes too large for him.

"Now then, what's the trouble?" inquired Ralph, when they were both seated on the water tank.

"Those men were pursuing me," said the lad.

"What for?"

"I was running away from them. They are my uncles, and they have been very wicked and cruel to me. They want to send me to a reform school to get rid of me, and locked me up. I ran away this morning, but they got trace of me again."

"What is your name?"

"Earl Danvers. My father died and left them my guardians. They are after the property, I guess."

"What do you propose to do?"

"Oh, anything to get away from them."

Ralph talked for quite a while with the boy and learned his entire history. Then he said:

"This is a case for a lawyer. Would you like to come to Stanley Junction with me and have a lawyer look into the matter for you?"

"No. I only want to escape from those bad men."

"That will follow. You come with me. I will interest myself in your case and see that you are protected."

"How kind you are—you are the only friend I ever knew," cried the boy, bursting into tears of gratitude.

Ralph took Earl Danvers home with him when they reached Stanley Junction. His kind-hearted mother was at once interested in the forlorn refugee. They managed to fit him out with some comfortable clothing, and Ralph told him to take a rest of a few days, when he would have him see their lawyer and tell him his story.

Two days later the young fireman reported at the roundhouse for duty, and the ensuing morning started on a new term of service as fireman of the Limited Mail.

The first trip out Griscom was engineer. Ralph noticed that he looked pale and worried. The run to the city was made in a way quite unusual with the brisk and lively veteran railroader. Ralph waited until they were on their way home from the roundhouse that evening. Then he said:

"Mr. Griscom, you have not been your usual self to-day."

"That's true, lad," nodded the engineer gravely.

"Anything the matter especially?"

"Oh, a little extra care on my mind and under the weather a bit besides," sighed Griscom.

"Can I help you in any way?" inquired Ralph.

"No, lad—we must all bear our own troubles."

The next day Griscom did not report for duty at train time. A man named Lyle was put on extra duty. Ralph did not know him very well nor did he like him much. He understood that he was a fine engineer but that he had been warned several times for drinking.

As he came into the cab, Ralph noticed that his eyes were dull and shifty, his hands trembled and he bore all the appearance of a man who had been recently indulging in liquor to excess.

As soon as they were out on the road, Lyle began to drink frequently from a bottle he took out of his coat. He became more steady in his movements, and, watching him, Ralph saw that he understood his business thoroughly and was duly attentive to it.

After the wait at the city, however, Lyle came aboard of the locomotive in quite a muddled condition. He was talkative and boastful now. He began to tell of the many famous special runs he had made, of the big salaries he had earned, and of his general proficiency as a first-class engineer.

He ordered full steam on, and by the time they were twenty miles from the city he kept the locomotive going at top notch speed. There was a tremendous head on the cylinders and they ran like a racer. Frogs and target rods were passed at a momentum that fairly frightened Ralph, and it was a wonder to him the way the wheels ground and bounded that they always lit on the steel.

Lyle took frequent drinks from the bottle, which had been replenished. His eyes were wild, his manner reckless, almost maniacal. As they passed signals he would utter a fierce, ringing yell. Ralph crowded over to him.

"Mr. Lyle," he shouted, "we are ahead of time."

"Good," roared the mad engineer, "I'm going to make the record run of the century."

"If any other train is off schedule, that is dangerous."

"Let 'em look out for themselves," chuckled Lyle. "Whoop! pile in the black diamonds."

"Stop!" almost shrieked Ralph.

Of a sudden he made a fearful discovery. A signal had called for a danger stop where the Great Northern crossed the tracks of the Midland Central. Unheeding the signal, Lyle had run directly onto a siding of the latter railroad and was traversing it at full speed.

"Stop, stop, I say—there's a car ahead," cried Ralph.

111

Lyle gave the young fireman a violent push backwards and forged ahead.

Chug! bang! A frightful sound filled the air. The locomotive had struck a light gondola car squarely, lifting it from the track and throwing it to one side a mass of wreckage. Then on, on sped the engine. It struck the main of the Midland Central.

Ralph grabbed up a shovel.

"Lower speed," he cried, "or I will strike you."

"Get back," yelled Lyle, pulling a revolver from his pocket. "Back, I say, or I'll shoot. Whoop! this is going."

Ralph climbed to the top of the tender. He was powerless alone to combat the engineer in his mad fury. A plan came into his mind. The first car attached to the tender was a blind baggage. Ralph sprang to its roof. Then he ran back fast as he could.

The young fireman lost no time, dropping from the roof between platforms. As he reached the first passenger coach he ran inside the car.

Passengers were on their feet, amazed and alarmed at the reckless flight of the train. The conductor and train hands were pale and frightened.

"What's the trouble?" demanded the conductor, as Ralph rushed up to him.

"A maniac is in charge of the train. He is crazed with drink, and armed. Who of you will join me in trying to overpower him?"

None of the train hands shrank from duty. They followed Ralph to the platform and thence to the top of the forward coach. At that moment new warnings came.

CHAPTER XXVII

A NEW MYSTERY

"Danger," shouted Ralph. "Quick, men. Do you see ahead there?"

Down the rails a red signal fuse was spluttering. It was quite a distance away, but they would reach it in less than sixty seconds if the present fearful speed of the train was kept up.

"Hear that?" roared the conductor in a hoarse, frightened tone.

Under the wheels there rang out a sharp crack, audible even above the roar of the rushing train—a track torpedo.

Ralph ran across the top of the forward car. As he reached its front end, Lyle turning discovered him.

He set up a wild yell, reached into the tender, seized a big sledgehammer lying there and braced back.

The young fireman was amazed and fairly terrified at his movements, for Lyle began raining blows on lever, throttle and everything in the way of machinery inside of the cab.

Past the red light, blotting it out, sped the train, turning a curve. Ralph anticipated a waiting or a coming train, but, to his relief, the rails were clear. Ahead, however, there was a great glow, and he now understood what the warnings meant.

The road at this point for two miles ran through a marshy forest, and this was all on fire. Ralph gained the tender.

"Back, back!" roared Lyle, facing him, weapon in hand. "She's fixed to go, can't stop her now. Whoop!"

With deep concern the young fireman noted the disabled machinery.

Half-way between centers, the big steel bar on the engineer's side of the locomotive had snapped in two and was tearing through the cab like a flail, at every revolution of the driver to which it was attached.

Just as Ralph jumped down from the tender, the locomotive entered the fire belt—in a minute more the train was in the midst of a great sweeping mass of fire. The train crew, blinded and singed, retreated. Ralph trembled at a sense of the terrible peril that menaced.

Lyle had drawn back from the lever or he would have been annihilated. Then as the fire swept into his face, he uttered a last frightful yell, gave a spring and landed somewhere along the side of the track.

The young fireman was fairly appalled. Such a situation he had never confronted before. The cab was ablaze in a dozen places. The tops of the cars behind had also ignited. Ralph did not know what to do. Even if he could have stopped the train, it would be destruction to do so now.

Suddenly the locomotive dove through the last fire stretch. Ahead somewhere Ralph caught the fierce blast of a locomotive shrieking for orders. For life or death the train must be stopped.

He flew towards the throttle but could not reach it safely. The great bar threatened death. Twice he tried to reach the throttle and drew back in time to escape the descending bar. At a third effort he managed to slip the latch of the throttle, but received a fearful graze of one hand. Then, exhausted from exertion and excitement, the young fireman saw the locomotive slow down not a hundred yards from a stalled train.

The passenger coaches were soon vacated by the passengers, while the train crew beat out the flames where the cars were on fire.

The Limited Mail made no return trip to Stanley Junction that night. The following morning, however, when the swamp fire had subsided, the train was taken back to the Great Northern and then to terminus.

Lyle, the engineer, was found badly burned and delirious in the swamp, where he would have perished only for the water in which he landed when he jumped from the locomotive cab. He was taken to a hospital.

There was a great deal of talk about the latest exploit of the young fireman of the Limited Mail, and Ralph did not suffer any in the estimation of the railroad people and his many friends.

One evening he came home from an interview with a local lawyer concerning the interests of his young friend, Earl Danvers.

Ralph felt quite sanguine that he could obtain redress for Earl from his heartless relations, and was thinking about it when he discovered his mother pacing up and down the front walk of the house in an agitated, anxious way.

"Why, mother," said Ralph, "you look very much distressed."

"I am so, truly," replied Mrs. Fairbanks. "Ralph, we have met with a great loss."

"What do you mean, mother?"

"The house has been burglarized."

"When?"

"Some time during the past three hours. I was on a visit to a sick neighbor, and returned to discover the rear door open. I went inside, and all the papers in the cabinet and some money we had there were gone."

"The papers?" exclaimed Ralph.

"Yes, every document concerning our claim against Gasper Farrington is missing."

"But what of Earl Danvers?" inquired Ralph. "Was he away from home?"

"He was when I left, but he must have returned during my absence."

"How do you know that?" asked Ralph.

"The cap he wore when he went away I found near the cabinet."

Ralph looked serious and troubled.

"I hope we have not been mistaken in believing Earl to be an honest boy," he said, and his mother only sighed.

Then Ralph began investigating. The rear door, he found, had been forced open. All the rooms and closets had been ransacked.

"This is pretty serious, mother," he remarked.

Earl Danvers did not return that day. This troubled and puzzled Ralph. He could not believe the boy to be an accomplice of Farrington, nor could he believe that he was the thief.

Next morning Ralph reported the loss to the town marshal. When he went down the road, he threw off a note where the men were working on the Short Line Route at its junction with the Great Northern. It was directed to Zeph Dallas, and in the note Ralph asked his friend to look up the two uncles of Earl Danvers and learn all he could about the latter.

It was two nights later when Mrs. Fairbanks announced to Ralph quite an important discovery. In cleaning house she had noticed some words penciled on the wall near the cabinet. They comprised a mere scrawl, as if written under difficulty, and ran:

"Earl prisoner. Two boys stealing things in house. Get the old coat I wore."

"Why, what can this mean?" said Ralph. "Earl certainly wrote this. A prisoner? two boys? the thieves? Get the old coat? He means the one he wore when he came here. What can that have to do with this business? Mother, where is the coat?"

"Why, Ralph," replied Mrs. Fairbanks, "I sold it to a rag man last week."

CHAPTER XXVIII

THE FREIGHT THIEVES

Two days later Zeph Dallas came to Stanley Junction to purchase some supplies for Mr. Gibson's construction camp. In the evening he called at the Fairbanks home. The farmer boy had located the relatives of Earl Danvers, and his report verified the story of the latter, who had disappeared from home, and, according to his uncles, his whereabouts was unknown to them.

Ralph related the story of the burglary, and Zeph was at once interested. He believed that some mystery of importance was attached to the old coat. When he had gone away Ralph got to thinking this over.

"Mother," he asked, "do you know the man to whom you sold that old coat?"

"Why, yes," replied Mrs. Fairbanks. "He is the man who goes around with an old wagon visiting the different country towns in this district in turn."

Ralph made some inquiries, and ascertained that the peddler in question made his headquarters at Dover. He resolved upon opportunity to visit the man at a near date, although it was probable that the coat with the rags sold with it had been sent to some mill. A few days later Zeph came again to Stanley Junction and Ralph told him about the peddler.

For a time after this, affairs ran on smoothly for the Limited Mail and her experienced crew, and Ralph had settled down to a quiet enjoyment of congenial employment when there occurred a break in the routine that once more placed him in a position of peril.

One day as he returned from the city run, the roundhouse foreman informed him that he was to report at the office of the master mechanic. Ralph did not go home, but went at once to answer the summons.

The master mechanic was his good friend and received him with his usual cordiality.

"Fairbanks," he said, "you are pretty well known to the officers of the road, and favorably, too, I suppose you know that."

"It is a pleasure to have you say so," answered the young fireman.

"They seem especially to value your ability in running down crookedness and ferreting out criminals," pursued the master mechanic. "The superintendent wired me today to have one road detective start out on a certain case. I wired back that Mr. Adair was engaged in a special case in the city. The return was to relieve you of regular duty and have you report at Afton this afternoon."

Ralph nodded to indicate that he understood, but he said:

"I do not like these interruptions to routine duty, but I suppose the company knows where it most needs a fellow."

Ralph went down the road shortly after noon. He reached Afton and reported at once to the assistant superintendent.

"I have ordered a substitute fireman on the Mail for a week, Fairbanks," said that official. "I think we shall engage your services for that length of time."

"Is it some particular case, sir?" asked Ralph.

"A very important case, yes. We seem to have got rid of incompetent employes and strikers, thanks to you and others who stood by the company in time of trouble. There is one thing, however, that is bothering us. It bothers every road more or less, but we won't have it."

Ralph waited for a further explanation.

"Freight thieves, Fairbanks," continued the official. "Some gang is regularly stealing from the road. When, where and how it is done we have been unable to ascertain. A train will leave the city or the Junction, arrive at terminus, and some valuable package will be missing. The car seals will be all right, no one seems to have entered the car, and yet the pilfering goes on. Will you help us run down the thieves?"

"I will try," answered Ralph. "What trains seem to suffer most?"

"Always the night freights," replied the assistant superintendent. "Now, take your time, spare no expense, and go to work on this problem in your usual effective way."

Ralph devoted the remainder of the day to going up and down the road and familiarizing himself with the various freight trains and their schedules.

Just after dark he clambered into the cab of the night freight leaving the city. It was a dark, sleety night, for cold weather had just set in.

The engineer was a tried and trusty veteran in the service. Ralph felt that he understood him, and that he must trust him to a degree in order to facilitate his own programme. He waited till the fireman was busy outside on the engine, then he spoke to the old engineer.

"Mr. Barton, I am on special duty here tonight."

"That so, lad?" inquired the engineer.

"Yes, I suppose you know there is a good deal of missing freight in these night runs."

"I heard so," answered Barton, "but you see that is the business of the conductor, so I haven't much troubled myself about it."

"Still, you don't care to have these things occur in your runs."

117

"Should say not! Working on the case, Fairbanks?"

"Frankly, yes, Mr. Barton, and I want you to keep it quiet, but assist me when you can. I will be all over the train and the car tops to-night, and wanted to explain why to you."

"That's all right, lad. Just call on me if I can help you. Hello, you, Woods!" bawled the engineer suddenly to a fellow who appeared near the cab side, "what you doing there?"

The man slunk out of view at being addressed, with a muttered remark that it was his own business.

"Don't like that fellow—caboose look-out," explained Barton.

"I hope he did not overhear our conversation," spoke Ralph.

About mid-way of the train there was a gondola oil car. It had an elevated runway so that train hands could pass over it readily. Ralph selected this car as a vantage point, and got aboard as the train started on its way for Stanley Junction.

He was dressed as a tramp, looked the character completely, and the false moustache he wore effectually changed his face so that no persons except familiar friends would easily recognize him.

Ralph got down at one side of the big oil tank. For the next hour he remained quiet. Finally, as a brakeman passed over the platform, he climbed up and kept track of his movements.

The man, however, simply passed up and down the train and then returned to the caboose. Then there was a stop. Ralph leaned from the car and looked up and down the train.

"Why," exclaimed Ralph suddenly, "there is that fellow Woods working at the doors of the cars a little ahead there."

The brakeman in question now came down the length of the train. The engine was taking water. He halted almost opposite the car Ralph was hiding on. Suddenly he uttered a low, sharp whistle, and it was answered. Three men appeared from the side of the track, spoke to him, bounded up on to the oil car, and crouched down so near to Ralph that he could almost touch them.

Woods stood on the next track with his lantern as if waiting for the train to start up.

"Cars marked," he spoke. "I'll flash the glim when the coast is clear. You'll know the cases I told you about."

There was no response. The locomotive whistled, and the brakeman ran back to the caboose. Ralph lay perfectly still. The three men sat up against the railing of the car.

"Got the keys to the car ventilators?" asked one of the men, finally.

"Sure," was the response. "Say, fellows, we want to be wary. This is a clever game of ours, but I hear that the railroad company is watching out pretty close."

"Oh, they can't reach us," declared another voice, "with Woods taking care of the broken seals, and all kinds of duplicate keys, we can puzzle them right along."

Just then one of them arose to his feet. He stumbled heavily over Ralph.

"Hello!" he yelled, "who is this?"

CHAPTER XXIX

A PRISONER

The three men almost instantly confronted Ralph, and one of them seized him, holding him firmly.

Ralph quickly decided on his course of action. He yawned in the face of the speaker and drawled sleepily:

"What are you waking a fellow up for?"

One held Ralph, another lit a match. They were rough, but shrewd fellows. Instantly one of them said:

"Disguised!" and he pulled off Ralph's false moustache. "That means a spy. Fellows, how can we tell Woods?"

"S—sh!" warned a companion—"no names. Now, young fellow, who are you?"

But "young fellow" was gone! In a flash Ralph comprehended that he was in a bad fix, his usefulness on the scene gone. In a twinkling he had jerked free from the grasp of the man who held him, had sprung to the platform of the oil car and thence to the roof of the next box car.

Almost immediately his recent captor was after him. It was now for Ralph a race to the engine and his friend Barton.

The running boards were covered with sleet and as slippery as glass, yet Ralph forged ahead. He could hear the short gasps for breath of a determined pursuer directly behind him.

"Got you!" said a quick voice. Its owner stumbled, his head struck the young fireman and Ralph was driven from the running board.

He was going at such a momentum that in no way could he check himself, but slid diagonally across the roof of the car. There destruction seemed to face him.

His pursuer had fallen flat on the running board. Ralph dropped flat also, clutching vainly at space. His fingers tore along the thin sheeting of ice. He reached the edge of the car roof.

For one moment the young fireman clung there. Then quick as a flash he slipped one hand down. It was to hook his fingers into the top slide bar of the car's side door. The action drew back the door about an inch. It was unlocked. Ralph dropped his other hold lightning-quick, thrust his hand into the interstice, pushed the door still further back, and precipitated himself forward across the floor of an empty box car.

There he lay, done up, almost terrified at the crowding perils of the instant, marveling at his wonderful escape from death.

"They must think I went clear to the ground," theorized Ralph. "I am safe for the present, at least. What an adventure! And Woods is in league with the freight thieves! That solves the problem for the railroad company.

"An empty car," he said, as he finally struggled to his feet. "I'll wait till the train stops again and then run ahead to Barton. Hello!" he exclaimed sharply, as moving about the car, his foot came in contact with some object.

Ralph stood perfectly still. He could hear deep, regular breathing, as of some one asleep. His curiosity impelled him to investigate farther. He took a match from his pocket, flared it, and peered down.

Directly in one corner of the car lay a big, powerful man. He was dressed in rags. His coat was open, and under it showed a striped shirt.

"Why!" exclaimed Ralph, "a convict—an escaped convict!"

The man grasped in one hand, as if on guard with a weapon of defense, a pair of handcuffs connected with a long, heavy steel chain. Apparently he had in some way freed himself from these.

Ralph flared a second match to make a still closer inspection of the man. This aroused the sleeper. He moved, opened his eyes suddenly, saw Ralph, and with a frightful yell sprang up.

"I've got you!" he said, seizing Ralph. "After me, are you? Hold still, or I'll throttle you. How near are the people who sent you on my trail?"

"I won't risk that," shouted the man wildly.

In a twinkling he had slipped the handcuffs over Ralph's wrists. The latter was a prisoner so strangely that he was more curious than alarmed.

"Going to stop, are they?" pursued the man, as there was some whistling ahead. "Mind you, now, get off when I do. Don't try to call, and don't try to run away, or I'll kill you."

The train stopped and Ralph's companion pulled back the door. He got out, forcing Ralph with him, and proceeded directly into the timber lining the railroad, never pausing till he had reached a desolate spot near a shallow creek.

Then the man ordered a halt. He sat down on the ground and forced his captive to follow his example.

"Who are you?" he demanded roughly.

"I am Ralph Fairbanks, a fireman on the Great Northern Railroad," promptly explained the young fireman.

"Do you know me?"

"I infer from these handcuffs and your under uniform that you are an escaped convict," answered Ralph.

"Know a good many people, do you?"

"Why, yes, I do," answered Ralph.

"Where is Stanley Junction?"

"About forty miles north of here. I live there."

"You do? you do?" cried the convict, springing up in a state of intense excitement. "Here, lad, don't think me harsh or mean, or cruel, but you have got to stay with me. You would betray me to the police."

"No, I would not," declared Ralph.

"You would, I know—it's human nature. There is a big reward out for me. Then, too, you know people. Yes, you must stay with me."

"I can't help you any—why should you detain me?" insisted Ralph.

"I must find a man," cried the convict, more wildly than ever—"or you must find him for me."

"What man is that?" spoke Ralph.

"Do you know a Mr. Gasper Farrington?"

"Quite well," answered Ralph, rather startled at the question.

"That is the man!" shouted the convict.

"And that is singular, for I am very anxious myself to find that same individual," said the young fireman.

Ralph felt that he was in the midst of a series of strange adventures and discoveries that might lead to important results, not only for the person he had so strangely met, but for himself, as well.

This impression was enforced as he watched his captor pace up and down the ground, muttering wildly. He seemed to have some deep-rooted hatred for Gasper Farrington. "Revenge," "Punishment," "Justice," were the words that he constantly uttered. Ralph wondered what course he could pursue to get the man down to a level of coherency and reason. Finally the man said:

"Come, get up, we must find some shelter."

After an hour of arduous tramping they came to an old barn that had been partly burned down. There was some hay in it. The convict lay down on this, unloosed one handcuff from the wrist of his prisoner, and attached the other to his own arm and lay as if in a daze until daybreak.

Now he could inspect his prisoner clearly, and Ralph could study the worn, frenzied face of his captor. The latter had calmed down somewhat.

"Boy," he said, finally, "I don't dare to let you go, and I don't know what to do."

"See here," spoke Ralph, "you are in deep trouble. I don't want to make you any more trouble. Suppose you tell me all about yourself and see if I can't help you out."

"Oh, I don't dare to trust any one," groaned the man.

"You spoke of Gasper Farrington," suggested Ralph. "Is he an enemy of yours?"

"He has ruined my life," declared the convict.

"And why do you seek him?"

"To demand reparation, to drag him to the same fate he drove me to. Just let me find him—that is all I wish—to meet him face to face."

Ralph began to quietly tell the story of his own dealings with the village magnate of Stanley Junction. It had a great effect upon his auditor. From dark distrust and suspicion his emotions gradually subsided to interest, and finally to confidence.

It was only by gradations that Ralph led the man to believe that he was his friend and could help him in his difficulties.

The convict told a pitiful story. Ralph believed it to be a true one. To further his own avaricious ends, Farrington had devised a villainous plot to send the man to the penitentiary. He had escaped. He had documents that would cause Farrington not only to disgorge his ill-gotten gains, but would send him to jail.

"I want to get to where those documents are hidden," said the convict. "Then to find Farrington, and I shall right your wrongs as well as my own."

Ralph reflected deeply over the matter in hand. He resolved on a course of proceedings and submitted it to his companion.

He offered to take the convict to the isolated home of Amos Greenleaf, where he could remain safely in retirement. Ralph promised to get him comfortable garments and provide for his board and lodging. In a few days he would see him again and help him to find Farrington.

The young fireman was now released from the handcuffs. He calculated the location of the place where Greenleaf lived.

"It is about fifteen miles to the spot I told you of," he explained to the convict.

"Can we reach it without being seen by any one?" anxiously inquired his companion.

"Yes, I can take a route where we need not pass a single habitation."

It was afternoon when they reached the home of old Amos Greenleaf.

Ralph experienced no difficulty in arranging that the convict remain there for a few days. He gave Greenleaf some money, and, promising to see the convict very soon, proceeded to Wilmer.

The young fireman took the first train for Afton, and reported what had occurred to the assistant superintendent.

Two days later Woods and his companions were in jail, and a great part of the stolen freight plunder was recovered.

Woods confessed that he had duplicated keys and seals for the doors and ventilators of the freight cars, and the bold thieveries along the Great Northern now ceased.

Ralph obtained leave of absence for a week. He decided that it was worth while to try and find Gasper Farrington. He went to the city, got certain papers belonging to the magnate from Mr. Grant, and went to Wilmer.

He was soon at the junction of the Springfield & Dover Short Cut Railroad and the Great Northern. That terminus was completed. A neat depot had been erected, and on the tracks of the new railroad there stood a handsome locomotive.

"Oh, Ralph!" cried Zeph Dallas, rushing forward to greet his friend, as the young fireman appeared. "Great news!"

CHAPTER XXX

THE LOST DIAMONDS

"Great news, eh?" said Ralph.

"You will say so when you hear what I have got to tell you," declared Zeph Dallas. "Say, I am going straight to headquarters. Come with me. The news will keep till we get there."

"All right," assented Ralph. "There is enough going on around here to keep a fellow interested."

"The new railroad?" spoke Zeph brightly. "I should say so. Isn't it just famous? I tell you, some hustling work has been done here in the past few weeks."

Ralph was amazed and delighted at the progress made by the Short Line Railway. As said, a new locomotive was on the rails at the terminus, and a little depot had been built. Workmen were busy as far down the line as he could see. In fact, everything indicated that the road would soon be in full operation.

"The tracks are laid both ways from headquarters, except for a little distance on the Springfield side," said Zeph. "We expect passenger and freight cars for the road to-day, and on Monday we open the line."

"And in what capacity will you appear on that grand occasion, Zeph?" inquired the young fireman pleasantly.

"Conductor!" exploded the farmer boy, drawing himself up proudly. "See here;" he drew back his coat and revealed the biggest and most elaborate "Conductor" badge manufactured. "We expect that Earl Danvers will become our brakeman."

"Who?" cried Ralph with a start.

"Earl Danvers."

"Is he here?"

"He is at headquarters," said Zeph. "Don't bother asking me about him now. You will soon see him, and he will tell you his own story. Then, too, Mr. Gibson wishes to see you particularly. Here's our hand-car, jump aboard. We'll spin along at a fine rate, I tell you, for the roadbed is splendid."

Ralph found it so. It was a most interesting journey to headquarters. There was only one track, and on this the men had spent their energies to great advantage, and commendable results followed.

He was warmly welcomed by his friends, particularly so by Earl Danvers. Just as soon as mutual greetings were over Ralph took Earl to a pile of ties a little distance away.

"Now then, young man," he said, "seeing we are alone, suppose you give an account of yourself."

Earl Danvers was thin and pale. He looked as if he had gone through some recent severe hardships, but he smiled serenely as he said:

"It's easy to tell my story, now I am out of my troubles, but I tell you, Ralph, I have had a hard time of it."

"With Slump and Bemis?"

"Yes. The afternoon I left Stanley Junction, they were the fellows who forced me to go away with them. They broke into your house, and I found them ransacking it. They pitched on to me, and tied me up. Then they recognized me."

"What, had you known them before?" exclaimed Ralph, in some surprise.

"I found out that I had. You remember the first day that you saw me?"

"Yes," nodded Ralph.

"Well, I had run away from my uncles that morning. I had made up a package hurriedly, containing shoes, coat and cap, and got away through a window in the attic. I went about five miles, when I ran right into two fellows in the woods. They were Slump and Bemis. They got mad at my stumbling over them, took away my parcel and began to belabor me. I had to run to keep from being terribly beaten. Then I sneaked around, hoping to recover my parcel. They had gone in swimming. My parcel had disappeared. I had to have a coat. I grabbed one and ran away with it. They yelled after me, but I outdistanced them. Then later I ran across my uncles looking for me. The rest you know."

"And what about the coat?"

"Well," related Earl, "when those fellows broke into your house, they inquired about that coat. I at once saw that they had a great interest in it. I told them I didn't know where it was. They insisted that I did. They ransacked the house from top to bottom. They took me away from town to a miserable hut where they were staying. Until yesterday I was a prisoner there, tied up, half-starved, and every day Slump would come and demand to know if I was going to tell him what had become of that coat. From the first I knew that coat was what they were after when they burglarized your house, and wrote what words I could on the wall of your sitting room."

"Yes," said Ralph, "we found your message there. Did you learn what their especial interest was in the coat?"

"Yes, I overheard some of their conversation a few days ago," replied Earl. "That coat contained some diamonds they found in an old box car."

"What!" cried Ralph. "Is it possible?"

"It seems so. I escaped yesterday. You had told me about this place, and so I came here. Zeph Dallas was my friend at once, when I told him my story. Here he is now."

Zeph approached with a beaming face.

"Fairbanks," he said, "I suppose Danvers has told you how he came here, and his troubles with Slump and Bemis."

"Yes," nodded Ralph.

"Well, I went to Dover yesterday and saw the old rag man. He ransacked his stock and we found the coat."

"You did?" spoke Ralph, expectantly.

"Yes, and in an inside pocket were the diamonds. Here they are."

Zeph handed Ralph a moldy chamois skin bag. With interest the young fireman inspected the contents.

"This is a rich find, Zeph," he said. "You must report to the car finder at once."

"I am going to the city to-day to see him," explained the former farmer boy.

Zeph left headquarters about noon. The next morning he reappeared. He was fairly gorgeous attired in the uniform of a conductor.

"One thousand dollars I get as a special reward for the recovery of the diamonds," he said, "and more when the car finder has seen their original owner. I am to divide with you, Fairbanks."

"Not at all," dissented Ralph.

"Oh, yes, I shall," insisted Zeph. "And, by the way, I have some news of importance for you."

"Indeed?" said Ralph.

"Yes. You know where Trafton is?"

"On the Midland Central."

"Exactly. Well, this morning on the platform there, I saw a man in whom you are considerably interested."

"Who was that?" inquired the young fireman.

"Bartlett, the fellow who was a partner of Gasper Farrington in that wire-tapping scheme."

CHAPTER XXXI

JUSTICE AT LAST—CONCLUSION

Ralph lost no time in making up his mind to at once go to Trafton and endeavor to run down Bartlett. He was the friend and confidant of Gasper Farrington, and the latter the young fireman was now determined to find.

He had his troubles for his pains. He got a trace of Bartlett at Trafton, but lost it again. His final clew was that Bartlett had last been seen driving away from town in a covered wagon.

Ralph devoted the morning to these discoveries, then he made for the home of Amos Greenleaf. He cut across the timber for ten miles, and late in the afternoon reached the miserable hovel where the crippled railroader lived.

It was when he was within a few rods of the place that a voice hailed him.

"This way, Mr. Fairbanks, I have something to tell you."

Ralph went to a copse near at hand where the speaker stood, as if in hiding. It was the escaped convict. He was deeply excited.

"I wanted to prepare you for a surprise before you went into the house," said the convict.

"Why, what do you mean?" asked Ralph.

"I mean Farrington!" cried the convict. "He is there."

"Impossible!" exclaimed Ralph.

"No, it is true."

"How did he happen to come here?"

"A man driving a covered wagon brought him. Farrington was sick, dying. The other man carried him into the house and said he would hurry for a doctor."

"When was this?" asked Ralph.

"Two hours ago. I have not shown myself to Farrington yet. The man is certainly in a dying condition."

"I had better investigate affairs," said Ralph, and he proceeded to the house.

Gasper Farrington lay on a wretched cot in a little bedroom. Ralph was amazed at the change in the magnate since he had last seen him. Farrington was thin, pale and weak. He was gasping painfully for breath, and groaned wretchedly as he recognized his visitor.

"Why, Mr. Farrington," said Ralph, "you are a very sick man."

"I am dying, Ralph Fairbanks," moaned the stricken Farrington. "You have your revenge."

"I wish for no revenge—I truly am sorry to see you in this condition."

"Well, here I am," groaned Farrington—"a miserable wreck, dying in a wretched hovel, the end of all my plotting, and worst of all, robbed of everything I own."

"By whom?" asked Ralph.

"By Bartlett, who has abandoned me. I know it, and only this morning he got from me the deeds conveying all my property to him. Once recorded, I am a beggar, and can make no reparation to those whom I have defrauded."

"Is that true?" asked Ralph.

"Yes. He pretended he would drive to Wilmer, record the deeds at Stanley Junction, return and take me safely out of the country. Instead, he has isolated me in this desolate place. Oh, to outwit him, Fairbanks!" continued the magnate eagerly. "I can yet defeat him if you can assist me."

"How?"

"Under the bed is my box of private papers. Unknown to Bartlett, last week, suspecting his scheme to rob me, believing I was dying, I executed deeds that distributed my property among those whom I had wronged. One deed is for your mother to adjust that twenty thousand dollar claim. Another is for a poor fellow I sent to jail—an innocent man. Another places my property in trust with your lawyer. Here they are," and Farrington took some documents from the box that Ralph had handed him. "Now then, act quickly."

Ralph looked over the papers. They were what the magnate described. He went outside and saw the convict, showing him the deed containing the name of "John Vance."

"Is that your name?" asked Ralph.

"It is," assented the convict.

"Then Farrington has done you tardy justice," and he explained the situation.

In a few minutes the young fireman was bounding away towards Wilmer.

Ralph caught a train just as it was moving away from the depot. He did not venture inside the cars, for he saw that Bartlett was aboard, but at the next station proceeded to the locomotive.

When the train reached the limits at Stanley Junction, Ralph left it and boarded an engine on another track bound for the depot.

He reached it some minutes in advance of the other locomotive. A hurried run for the office of the recorder, a swift delivery of the deeds, and then Ralph hastened after the town marshal.

They came upon Bartlett leaving the office of the recorder with a glum and puzzled face. In his hand in a listless way he held some deeds which he had evidently been told were worthless.

The man was disguised, but Ralph knew him at once. The marshal stepped forward and seized his arm.

"Mr. Bartlett," he said sternly, "you are under arrest."

"Oh, you want me? What—er—for?" stammered the plotter.

"Conspiracy in the recent railroad strike," explained the official. "Pretty serious, too—not to mention that so-called accident you had on one of the cars, for which you wanted damages."

With a scowl on his face Bartlett turned and confronted Ralph.

"Ah, so it's you?" he growled.

"Yes," returned the young fireman, coldly.

"This is some of your work!"

"If so, it is at the request of the man you robbed, Bartlett."

"Eh?"

"I mean Gasper Farrington," answered Ralph, and this news caused the prisoner to turn pale and stagger back. He realized that he had come to the end of his plotting and must now suffer the consequences of his misdeeds. He was marched off to jail, and it may be as well to state, was, later on, sent to prison for a term of years.

Gasper Farrington did not linger long. Before he died, however, he had a talk with Ralph and with the convict, and signed several papers of importance. He acknowledged all his wrong doings, and did all in his power to straighten matters out. His relatives came to his aid, and his last hours on earth were made as comfortable as circumstances permitted.

Two days after Farrington's funeral came a surprise for Ralph. He received word that Ike Slump and Mort Bemis had been caught in a tavern near Dover. Both of the roughs were in rags and penniless, having lost what money they had had. Both were turned over to the police, and in due course of time each followed Bartlett to prison.

"It serves them right," said Griscom, to Ralph. "My! my! What a difference in boys! Do you remember when you and Slump were both wipers at the roundhouse?"

"I do indeed!" answered Ralph feelingly. "I am sorry for Ike. But he has no one to blame but himself."

"A holiday for us day after to-morrow, lad," went on the veteran engineer of the Limited Mail, with a twinkle in his eye. "Guess you know why."

"Opening of the other line?" queried the young fireman.

"Exactly. Special invitation for both of us," went on Griscom, with a chuckle.

"Well, I hope everything pans out right," said Ralph. "Our friends have worked hard enough, goodness knows."

The day for the opening of the new railroad came, and Ralph and the old engineer took the early morning train for Wilmer. Not a few friends accompanied them.

"It's a great day for Van and for Mr. Gibson," said Ralph. "And a great day for Zeph and Earl too," he added, with a smile. Earl's uncles had been hailed into court, and a new guardian had been appointed for the boy.

A little after noon that day the formal opening of the Springfield & Dover Railroad was celebrated.

Two beautiful passenger coaches were filled with friends of the road and persons living near Wilmer. The locomotive and cars were gaily decorated with bunting. Limpy Joe was bustling around his restaurant stand at the depot, happy and chipper. Zeph Dallas was the proud conductor, and Earl Danvers the brakeman of the train. Mr. and Mrs. Gibson, Mrs. Fairbanks, Mr. Trevor and some of their friends formed a party by themselves. It was a regular gala occasion. The first trip was a grand success. People along the line greeted the train with glad cheers, and, returning to headquarters, a sumptuous repast was spread for the guests of the new road.

"Well, we are a happy family party," said Farwell Gibson with enthusiasm, as, that evening, his employes sat around the supper table at headquarters.

"Yes," nodded Trevor. "To-morrow actual work begins. We have splendid prospects, loyal employes, and the Springfield & Dover Short Line is a grand success."

"I cannot too deeply announce my feelings towards you, Fairbanks," said Mr. Gibson. "It is to your friendship and co-operation that I owe, in a measure, all my good fortune in completing the railroad."

"A grand lad," applauded old John Griscom heartily. "His pluck and perseverance have helped us all out of difficulties many a time."

"Three cheers for the boy who helped to build a railroad!" cried Zeph Dallas.

They were given with enthusiasm, and Ralph had to respond with a speech.

"I believe this is the happiest moment of my life," he declared. "I have been through some strenuous times, but all has ended well."

And then what a cheer went up!

Ralph imagined that now, since his enemies had been disposed of, quiet times were ahead. But this was not to be. Adventures in plenty still awaited him, and what some of them were will be related in another story, to be called "Ralph on the Overland Express; or, The Trials and Triumphs of a Young Engineer."

"It was certainly a great day, mother," said the young fireman, when he got home from the celebration.

"Yes, Ralph," answered Mrs. Fairbanks. "And to think that you helped to make that day possible. Oh, I am proud of you!" And she gave him a fond caress.

"And the best of it is, that we have all those thousands of dollars," continued the young fireman. "We are not exactly rich, but we are comfortably situated, eh?"

"Yes, indeed, Ralph! But listen to me. Do you want to leave the railroad? You might go into business, or go to college, or—"

"No, no, mother! I was born to follow a railroad life—I feel it. Who knows, some day I may be the President of some road."

"That is true. Well, have your wish, Ralph. They tell me now you are the best fireman in these parts. Soon you'll have your engine then—"

"I'll be very happy!" finished Ralph.

And his eyes brightened as he thought of splendid opportunities the future promised.

THE END

Milton Keynes UK
Ingram Content Group UK Ltd.
UKHW010652140923
428670UK00004B/245

9 791041 825752